HURRICANE FORCE

A Miss Fortune Mystery

NEW YORK TIMES BESTSELLING AUTHOR
JANA DELEON

Chapter One

I was in the middle of a particularly awesome raspberry pastry and the strongest cup of coffee ever when my cell phone rang. It was 7:00 a.m., so I knew before I looked at the display that only a handful of names might show. I sighed with relief when I saw Ally's name. Of the three who would call me this early, she was the least likely to have an emergency requiring risk of life or exposure. And since Ally was the one who'd provided me with the particularly awesome raspberry pastry, I was happy to help with whatever she had going on first thing on a Monday morning.

"You have to get down here," Ally said a split second after I answered.

"What's up?"

"Uncle Max is eating breakfast at the café and Aunt Celia always has breakfast here Monday morning. There's certain to be fireworks."

"On my way!"

Ida Belle and Gertie's archenemy, Celia Arceneaux, was the new mayor of Sinful, although the election was currently under investigation. One of her first moves as mayor had been dismissing the old sheriff from his position and replacing him with her cousin, who was busted two days ago for dealing meth. Celia's stock in Sinful was plummeting rapidly, and the appearance of her long-assumed-dead husband was certain to put an even bigger dent in her already-scarred reputation.

I jumped up from the table, grabbed my car keys, and wrapped the pastry in a paper towel, then rushed outside and jumped in my Jeep. I called Ida Belle and Gertie as I alternated driving and eating the pastry with my other hand. Ida Belle was standing at the curb when I pulled up. She swung into the passenger's seat with a flexibility and speed that defied her age and we took off around the corner for Gertie.

Gertie was also waiting at the curb…halfway up a ladder.

"What the heck?" I yelled and pointed as I approached.

"Hurry up!" Gertie yelled. "Just drive by and I'll jump in. It will save time."

"Good God," Ida Belle mumbled.

I could imagine about fifty ways this wasn't going to turn out well and not a single one in which it did, but I slowed down and pulled over as close to the curb as possible, praying that she didn't land on the hood. Or Ida Belle. I'd never hear the end of that one.

As I inched closer, Gertie motioned me forward with her hand, looking slightly exasperated at my slow pace. I didn't want to insult her, but at the same time, I knew better than to go any faster. Gertie was a good fifty years and a decent set of balance and vision away from auditioning for Cirque du Soleil. As I pulled alongside, Ida Belle leaned toward the center of the Jeep, bracing herself for the potential of being Gertie's air bag. Gertie bent her knees slightly, preparing for the leap, and as I pulled up beside her, she went for it.

Straight backward.

Apparently, there had been a little too much spring in her push-off and she'd managed to shove the ladder forward, which in turn propelled her backward. As the ladder fell toward the Jeep, I floored it so that it wouldn't hit us, looking behind me the entire time as Gertie flew off the ladder and onto the sidewalk.

Unfortunately, the sidewalk wasn't empty. A girl, probably twelve or so, and her German shepherd were in the wrong place at the wrong time. Gertie crashed into the girl, causing her to drop her leash. At the same time, the door to the house next door flew open and a woman stepped out holding a cat.

"What the heck is going on out here?" the woman shouted.

The German shepherd zeroed in on the cat and took off like a shot. The girl leaped up from the sidewalk and ran after the dog. The cat, sensing impending doom, shot over the woman's shoulder and back into the house. The woman managed to get the screen door closed as the dog jumped onto the porch, but it didn't slow him one bit. He went right through the screen and into the house, the woman screaming behind him.

Gertie jumped up from the sidewalk and crawled into the Jeep, falling onto the floorboard, as the sound of breaking glass echoed from the house. "Haul butt!" Gertie yelled.

"What about the ladder and the dog?" I asked.

"I don't like Dorothy or that cat, and the ladder doesn't belong to me."

The explanation was missing a few key elements, like whether Dorothy would press charges and who the ladder belonged to, but I wasn't sure I wanted the answers. It reeked of complication. I punched the accelerator down and the Jeep lurched forward.

Ida Belle turned to look behind us. "That's *my* ladder!"

Well, that was one question answered. I wheeled around the corner, hoping Dorothy had bad eyesight and wasn't calling her lawyer.

Gertie crawled onto the seat. "You can buy another ladder."

"I already did," Ida Belle said. "You borrowed that one ten years ago."

"Then it doesn't matter, now, does it?"

Ida Belle's expression said differently, but she must have decided it was a lost cause. "So what's the emergency?" she asked me.

I relayed Ally's phone call.

"Drama!" Gertie yelled and bounced up and down on the seat like a five-year-old.

Ida Belle narrowed her eyes at me. "You're getting good at this inside information thing. Usually I hear about everything first."

"Well, Ally's living with me, so I guess that gives me the edge in this case. Did you find out anything last night from the Sinful Ladies about Max's big return?"

Ida Belle shook her head. "All of Celia's friends are as surprised as we were, and it seems to everyone that Celia is just as shocked as the rest of us. She's not a good actor, so that part is probably true."

"When Max disappeared, all that he took were his clothes and his truck, right? Did she look for him or report him missing?" I asked.

"Oh, yes," Ida Belle said. "The state police were called in when he didn't come home after a week, but they didn't find anything. No money gone from the bank account, no use of credit cards, no one had seen him in his usual haunts, and his boat was in the slip we stole it from."

I cringed. "We should probably keep that last bit on the down low since the boat's real owner has returned from the dead."

"And since we sank the boat," Gertie said.

"I'm pretty sure I remember that part," I said. "So what was it like when Max disappeared?"

"It was like he was abducted by aliens," Gertie said. "One

minute he was there, and the next, he was simply gone."

"The police had no reason to suspect foul play," Ida Belle said, "and I imagine once they met Celia, they had a good idea why Max had chosen that form of exit."

"But I thought Celia's cousin said they had divorced," I said.

"I never believed that," Gertie said. "I think Celia told that lie because the truth was more embarrassing. Who wants to admit they are so awful that their husband gave up his entire identity and a darned nice cabin cruiser to get away?"

"Good point," I said. "So what did people think happened? I mean, when Marie's husband disappeared, everyone assumed she'd killed him, but I've never heard anyone suggest that with Celia. Burning his clothes and dumping his truck in the bayou wouldn't have been hard to stage."

"Marie's husband was rich," Ida Belle said. "Max was a loser who fancied himself an artist. He could do a decent imitation of other work but didn't have an ounce of vision himself. Hardly going to set the world on fire that way. Celia had some money of her own…inherited, so not something Max could get his hands on. She'd been smart and always kept it separate from marital assets."

"So what was the gossip?" I asked.

"Some people thought he'd stopped off at a bar on his way out of town, gotten drunk, and wandered off into the swamp and drowned," Gertie said. "He was a pretty good drinker. He *was* married to Celia. And if his truck was parked in the same spot in a bar parking lot for a couple days, someone would have lifted it. Unless someone's shooting at them, no one that works in a bar would call the cops."

"I could see that," I said. "And I know that you don't always find a body in the bayou, but now that we know he's alive, what does everyone think? I mean, he had to be living somewhere, and last time I checked, you couldn't do that on unoriginal artwork. He had to have a job and couldn't have been using his own ID or the state police would have found him in a matter of days. The man was gone over twenty years."

"Exactly," Ida Belle said. "That's what makes the entire thing so interesting. I mean, I know plenty of people live off-grid, but it takes some doing to manage it well. Max never struck me as all that clever, but maybe we were wrong."

I pulled onto Main Street, musing over the mystery that was Maxwell Arceneaux. I had a feeling that a whole bunch of interesting things were about to come out.

"After all these years," I said, "Max didn't come out of hiding for no reason. He has an agenda."

"Oh yeah," Ida Belle agreed.

Gertie clapped. "I can't wait to see what it is!"

I pulled into a parking spot in front of the café and we hurried inside. A man sat alone at a table in the back. I knew it was Max because I'd never seen him before and because everyone in the café kept shooting glances in his direction, but no one made a move to speak to him.

Five feet eleven, two hundred eighty pounds, less muscle content than a newborn, only a threat to the pancakes in front of him.

Ida Belle hurried to a table in the middle of the café and we took seats. "This should give us the best view of the showdown," she said, and checked her watch. "Celia should be here any minute."

Ally hurried over with coffee, her face flushed. "This feels so weird," she said, her voice low. "I was too young to remember Uncle Max well, but I felt too uncomfortable to wait on him. I made Francine do it."

"Did she get anything out of him?" Gertie asked.

Ally shook her head. "Nothing but his breakfast order. And she tried. You know Francine."

Gertie's eyes widened. "Francine is like the KGB and a Jedi knight. If she couldn't get anything out of him, then he's really clammed up."

I glanced around the café, which was suspiciously busy for a Monday morning. "I think word is spreading," I said.

Gertie nodded. "This is the most exciting thing to happen in Sinful in, well..."

"A day or two?" I finished.

Gertie grinned. "Got me there, but given that this is about Celia, and there's the election hoopla besides, this is the best nonlethal thing that's happened in a while."

"It's not lethal yet," Ida Belle said.

Gertie looked out the front glass window and smacked me on the arm. "Here she comes."

The low buzz that had filled the café disappeared like the wind, leaving only silence in its wake. Ally froze in place next to me, like one of those figures in Madame Tussauds. Not even the rattle of a spoon came from the kitchen. I glanced over at the swinging door and saw three sets of eyes peering out of the crack. Francine stood at the front of the restaurant next to a table of fishermen, holding a coffeepot.

The entire café of people locked their gazes on the front door as the bell jangled and Celia walked in. I glanced at the back corner as Max stabbed a forkful of pancakes, apparently the only person unfazed by Celia's arrival. Which made it even more interesting.

Celia stopped short as the door closed behind her and looked around the restaurant. "What's wrong?" she asked. "Is my slip showing?"

All heads turned slightly to look at the man in the back

corner. He'd polished off the pancakes and was now tearing into a slice of ham. Celia caught sight of her husband and sucked in a breath.

"You!" she said. "What are you doing here?"

Max looked up from his breakfast, his expression one of complete and utter boredom. "Eating." He dropped his head back down and went to work on the ham again.

Celia's face flushed red and her hands shook.

I leaned toward Gertie. "Is she packing?"

"I hope not," Gertie said. "I don't want to hit the floor in these slacks."

"You already hit the sidewalk."

"Oh yeah. I forgot."

Celia stomped to the back of the café. I watched her hands carefully. "She's not reaching into her purse," I said. "That's a good sign."

"It's a café," Gertie whispered. "No shortage of knives."

"I can outrun a knife."

Celia stopped in front of Max's table and glared down at him. "What are you doing in Sinful?"

"This is my hometown," Max said. "I can't visit my hometown?"

His tone was slightly mocking, and I waited for Celia's head to spin around and pop off her body.

"No," Celia said. "You can't just visit your hometown when you abandoned it and everyone in it years ago. Not even a phone call or a letter. Nothing to let anyone know you were still alive."

"That was sorta the whole idea."

"You didn't even come to your daughter's funeral!"

Max smirked, and I decided right then that no matter how much I disliked Celia, I disliked Max even more. There was something about his entire demeanor that was all off. Celia was a complete bitch and being married to her was probably like walking through the valley of the shadow of death, but behind that smirk was something else. Something cruel.

"Are you still passing off that old lie?" Max asked. "We both know Pansy was no kin of mine."

There was a sharp intake of breath and I looked over at Ida Belle and Gertie, who looked back at me and gave me a slight headshake. Holy crap, this was getting good. If Pansy wasn't Max's biological daughter and not even Gertie and Ida Belle knew about it, then Max's return was going to be like an earthquake hitting Sinful, right underneath Celia's house.

Celia turned practically purple and started to sputter. "You should have stayed away. No one wants you here."

"Yeah, well, I've come to collect what's mine."

"What's yours?" Celia's voice shot up several octaves. "Nothing here is yours. You gave it all up when you left."

"That might be what you think, but the legal system thinks differently. We bought that house together, so half the equity in it is mine, and there's my boat."

"Your damned boat sank! And good luck getting half the equity in the house. Last time I checked, the legal system didn't award settlements to dead people."

Max's eyes widened a bit.

"That's right," Celia continued. "I had you declared legally dead, and as far as I'm concerned, that's the status you'll keep."

"Is that a threat?"

"I suppose it is." Celia whirled around and stalked out of the café, letting the door slam shut behind her. A second later, the entire café erupted in excited conversation.

"Holy crap," I said. "Pansy wasn't his daughter? Did you have any idea?"

Ida Belle and Gertie shook their heads.

"Do you think it's even true?" I asked.

"She didn't argue the point," Ida Belle said, "and she looked like she was going to pass out, so yeah, I'd say it's a definite possibility."

Gertie cringed. "I can't believe more than one man slept with her. Ick. Celia always claimed Pansy was born early, but she went to New Orleans to have her and stayed for a month. She said Pansy had to stay in the hospital, but when she finally got back to Sinful, the baby looked plenty big to me. Of course, the thought crossed my mind that she might have been pregnant before she got married. The wedding was a bit of a rush job, but I never once thought that Max wasn't Pansy's father."

"I can't believe something that big never got out," I said.

Ally frowned. "When we were kids, Pansy said something to me once about her 'real' father. I thought she was pretending, you know, since Uncle Max had run off and all, but maybe she knew or suspected, anyway."

"Did she say who it was?" Ida Belle asked.

Ally shook her head. "Just something about Aunt Celia and a trip to San Francisco."

Ida Belle and Gertie looked at each other. "You don't think?" Gertie said.

"What?" Ally said. "Do you know what that means?"

Ida Belle whipped out her phone. "Celia had family out there that she used to visit—an aunt and some cousins—but she stopped going after she graduated from high school."

"That's right," Gertie said. "Of course, it didn't mean anything back then. She married Max and they settled down in Sinful, so nothing to set off alarms."

"Got it!" Ida Belle turned her phone around and showed us a high school yearbook picture of a man.

A man who looked a whole lot more like Pansy than Max

did.

"Who is that?" I asked.

Ida Belle smiled. "The aunt's husband."

"Holy crap!" Ally shouted, then slapped her hand over her mouth. She glanced around the café, then leaned in. "Celia had an affair with her uncle? What the hell is wrong with my family?"

Gertie frowned. "I don't know as I'd call it an affair. The uncle had to be in his midforties at the time, and Celia was only eighteen. I know women are a lot more knowledgeable about things these days, but back then, a man that age could have pulled a fast one on an impressionable young woman. And Celia's mother was strict. She had no street smarts to speak of."

"That's true enough," Ida Belle said, "and if you consider that Celia never had much in the way of male attention, then it's a recipe for being taken advantage of."

"So if Celia was pregnant with another man's child, why did Max marry her?" I asked.

Ida Belle shook her head. "That is a damned good question."

"I think we should mull it over with some blueberry pancakes," Gertie said.

I nodded. "That's the best idea I've heard in a long time."

"Make a note," Ida Belle said. "Her next idea is sure to be a doozy."

Chapter Two

As we exited the café, Deputy Carter LeBlanc ran out of the sheriff's department. In his jeans and black T-shirt, with his rugged good looks and awesome body, he looked as if he'd stepped off of one of those law enforcement hottie calendars. I felt my entire body stir and my heart leap more than just a little. Carter had become one of the biggest surprises I'd encountered since I'd arrived in Sinful. He was also my biggest dilemma.

He caught sight of us and hurried across the street, frowning. As he approached, I raised my right hand. "I swear, whatever it is, we didn't do it. We were just having breakfast and watching the Celia and Max show."

"Ah man," Carter said. "Celia and Max had a showdown? I can't believe I missed it. What happened?"

"Max basically said Pansy wasn't his daughter," I said.

Carter's eyes widened. "Really?"

"Scout's honor," Gertie said.

"You weren't a Scout," Ida Belle said.

"Only because they wouldn't let girls in," Gertie said. "Anyway, Max wouldn't say why he came back or where he's been all this time, and Francine had a crack at him before Celia got there."

Carter looked impressed. "If Francine couldn't get it out of him, he must really be up to something big. We could have used her in Iraq."

"So if you weren't coming over here to accuse us of something that I'm certain we would never do, why were you frowning?" I asked.

"The hurricane," he said.

"Crap."

"I knew it."

Ida Belle and Gertie both spoke at once.

"What?" I asked, completely confused.

"Tropical Storm Lizzie turned into a hurricane in the wee hours of the morning," Ida Belle said. "It was headed for Mobile, but apparently, it's shifted."

Carter nodded. "Looks to come in somewhere between New Orleans and Gulfport."

I felt a bit of panic course through me. Desert storms, assassins, and incendiary devices I could deal with. Hurricanes were outside of my scope. "Do we need to evacuate?"

"No," Ida Belle said. "If it comes in that far east, we'll just get flash flooding and a tornado or two."

"Sounds like a good reason to leave to me," I said.

"If we left every time there was a threat of flooding and tornadoes," Gertie said, "no one would live here at all."

"Seriously?" I looked at the three of them. "I've been living in a constant state of weather peril and none of you thought you should fill me in?"

Carter raised one eyebrow. "Given the things you've involved yourself in since arriving in Sinful, I'm going to go out on a limb and say even if the hurricane hit Sinful directly, it would be a better bet than some of the other choices you've made."

I frowned. It wasn't exactly untrue, but it was slightly rude of him to point it out while I was having my moment of panic. "Fine," I said, relaxing. "If you guys say there's nothing to worry about, then I won't worry. What do I need to do to prepare, boil water or something?"

"Only if you're delivering a baby," Gertie said, "which happened during a hurricane a couple years back."

"You delivered a baby?" Suddenly, it all became scary again.

"I tried asking him to stay in there for another day," Gertie said, "but babies can be stubborn that way."

"She really did ask," Ida Belle said. "Pleaded, actually."

"I don't blame her," I said. "Okay, so baby delivering aside, what do I need to do?" My mind whirled with all the things in Marge's house. Did I board up windows? Did I have enough beer to last out the storm? What if the power went out? Could Ally make blueberry muffins over a campfire? And what would I build a campfire out of? I didn't like the fig tree much, but it was live wood. It probably wouldn't burn very well.

"It's simple," Ida Belle said. "You close the storm shutters and secure them, fill the bathtubs with water, make sure you have flashlights and batteries, and that's it."

"Why are we taking baths?" I asked.

Carter laughed. "If we lose utilities, you'll need the water to flush toilets."

"Unless you want to fish it out of the bayou," Gertie said. "Plenty of people do."

"No thanks." I'd seen what lived in the bayou and didn't want any of it near places my naked butt rested. "So I batten down the hatches and ride it out? That's it?"

"Oh, you can't stay at your house when the storm hits shore," Ida Belle said. "You're right on the bayou, and there's a chance the bayou could come inside your kitchen. Everyone with property on water goes to one of the churches. Gertie and I handle those staying at the Baptist church and Celia and her group handle those staying at the Catholic church."

"Just when I thought I'd gotten out of going to church this week," I grumbled.

"Pastor Don's visiting his sister, so there won't be any preaching," Gertie said. "But I can't promise no singing or prayer. People tend to get worried when the storm hits."

Yeah. I was right there with them.

"We best get to the store and get more batteries before the rush," Ida Belle said.

"I'll catch up with you guys later," Carter said. "I'm on my way to the fire department to get the storm alarm set off." He gave me a quick kiss, then hurried off down the street.

Gertie reached into her purse and brought out three sets of earplugs. "You want to put these on. Trust me."

Ida Belle took a pair and popped them in her ears. "She's right," she yelled. "That siren is horribly loud. Sounds like a dinosaur-sized cat wailing."

I stuck one earplug in and nodded. I already needed them if Ida Belle was going to keep yelling.

We headed across the street to the General Store. Walter was in his usual spot behind the counter, reading the newspaper. He looked up when we came in and nodded. "Figured you'd be in when you heard the news. I put together a box of supplies for the church. It's sitting by the hat rack. I'll have Scooter run it over for you as soon as you check and make sure you don't need anything else."

"We need batteries!" Ida Belle yelled.

Walter winced and I waved an earplug at him.

"Ah," he said. "Carter's going to get the siren set off." He pulled out a pair of earmuffs and put them on. "I still have to hear customers, but at least the muffs take the edge off." He motioned Ida Belle and Gertie toward the box he'd referred to before and they set off across the store to check it out.

"Take those off for a minute," I said.

"What?" Walter yelled.

I reached up and yanked the muffs off his head. "I don't want to yell."

"Probably just as well. It usually takes them forever to get that alarm on, and it's hard to wait on people when you can't hear a word they're saying."

"You heard about Max, right?"

"Oh yeah. Two of the fishermen came hurrying over here yesterday after he showed up, then Celia came in this morning, ranting like a crazy woman. That part was nothing new, mind you, but she did buy a box of shotgun shells."

"Did she say why?"

"Claimed she needed to protect her home. I guess she thinks Max is going to break in."

"And she thinks shooting him is a good answer for that?" My mind whirled with all the legal possibilities. Was it breaking and entering if you used to own the home, were supposed to be dead, and it turned out you were just a butthole who left your wife and didn't bother to tell her for twenty years? If Celia shot him breaking into her—their house, was it self-defense or murder one?

"A bit of a messy situation Celia's in," Walter said, cluing in on my thoughts.

"I'll say. I have no idea what would happen if she shot him."

Walter nodded. "Can't say that I know myself. I'm just hoping we don't have to find out."

"Did you know Max well?"

"Not really, but then I don't think anyone did except Celia. Turns out, she probably didn't know him that well either, I guess. Max was always a loner. Most people considered him a bit odd.

He was always wandering around with a sketch pad, drawing odd renditions of buildings and people. It put people off the way he'd stare at them, then start marking on that pad."

"I can imagine." I wouldn't want someone sketching me without permission. It was creepy.

"Why do you ask?"

"Because I figure if he came back after all these years, it's for a darned good reason, and so far, no one can give me one."

"I don't think anyone's got a good reason to give."

"Except Max."

"I suppose he does, but I'd bet he's not going to share it. Not until he's ready."

"I'm sure you're right. I guess we'll just hope he's not here to try to rob Celia."

"Hope and pray on that one," Walter said. "The woman is a horrible shot. She'd probably end up shooting a neighbor."

I cringed. "We should probably warn Marie." Ida Belle and Gertie's good friend lived next door to Celia.

Walter nodded, then looked up at the door as the bells jangled. "Uh-oh. Speak of the devil."

"He's here?" I struggled not to whirl around and stare.

"Coming this way," Walter mumbled.

I heard the footsteps behind me and Walter looked past me. "Max," Walter said. "What can I do for you?"

"I heard the storm's moving in," Max said. "Figured I better get a flashlight and some water."

Unable to stand it any longer, I turned around and stuck my hand out. "I don't think we've met. I'm Sandy-Sue Morrow, Marge Boudreaux's niece." I threw out my cover identity like a pro and gave myself silent props for not cringing when I said the name "Sandy-Sue."

Max shook my hand. "How's old Marge doing?"

"She's dead. I'm here this summer settling her estate."

Max looked a bit taken aback at the directness of my response, but he recovered quickly. "I'm sorry to hear that. She was quite a character."

"That she was. So I hear through the grapevine that you've been gone for some time. What brings you back to town?"

Max's expression went completely blank. "Just a bit of unfinished business. Shouldn't take long to clear it up, then Celia can scramble to salvage what's left of her flagging reputation and try to lord over the masses once more."

"You really don't like your wife, do you?" I asked.

Walter snorted and reached for a tissue, trying to pretend he was coughing.

Max smiled. "No one likes my wife. Why should I be any different?"

"I don't know, because you married her?"

"The biggest mistake of my life, and one I fixed as soon as I had the ability to."

I frowned. Sure, Celia was a raging bitch and a perpetual thorn in the side of anyone with a lick of common sense, but no one deserved such disdain from the person they'd made vows with. My initial assessment of Max had been correct. He wasn't a nice man.

The bells on the door jangled again, and a gray-haired woman walked in holding hands with a man, probably twenty years younger than her. The younger man shared the same facial features, but his head remained dropped, his gaze locked on the floor. I could tell that he wasn't completely right. I didn't even bother with my usual assessment. There was nothing to fear here.

"Morning, Mrs. Hinkley," Walter said. "Will you and Landon be needing some hurricane supplies?"

Mrs. Hinkley cast a glance at Max and wrinkled her nose, as if she'd smelled something unpleasant, then gave Walter a nod. "Some batteries, kerosene, and a couple jugs of drinking water, please."

Walter reached for a box and set off in the store to assemble Mrs. Hinkley's supplies. Max gave Mrs. Hinkley a nod and looked at the young man.

"Hello, Landon," Max said. "Do you remember me? You used to draw pictures for me."

Landon finally lifted his gaze and stared at Max for a moment, then moved behind his mother. "No! No drawing! No more!"

Max's eyes widened. "I'm sorry," he rushed to say.

Mrs. Hinkley turned around and rubbed her hand up and down Landon's arm. "It's okay," she said, her voice calm and soft. "You don't have to draw. I've got a new can of clay for you."

Some of the tension left Landon's shoulders and he looked up at her. "Is it blue?"

"Of course it's blue," she said. "Isn't that your favorite color?"

Landon nodded. "I like blue."

"Why don't you see if you can help Walter," Mrs. Hinkley said, then turned around again as Landon headed off across the store.

"I didn't mean to upset him," Max said.

"It wasn't you," Mrs. Hinkley said. "He's been that way ever since I brought him back to Sinful from the group home. He loves making animals out of clay, but he won't pick up a pencil at all. I'm sure it's a phase of some sort."

Max frowned. "That's unfortunate. He always loved drawing. Of course, I haven't seen him in a long time. I guess things change."

"They certainly do," Mrs. Hinkley said, but her tone had grown frosty.

Max took the hint and gave us a nod. "I best go get my supplies. Good day, ladies."

Mrs. Hinkley waited until Max had walked away, then looked over at me. "You must be Marge's niece. I've heard a lot about you."

"All good, I hope," I joked.

She smiled. "Mostly. Except for the stuff Celia said, but then I stopped paying attention to what Celia says sometime shortly after my birth."

I nodded. "I like a smart woman."

She laughed. "Then we should get along fine. You in here for supplies?"

"Yep." I pointed to Ida Belle and Gertie, who were going through a box of supplies in the corner. "I'm depending on them for direction. This is my first hurricane."

"Well, you've got the best helping you out. Ida Belle and Gertie are part of Sinful's emergency management team for hurricanes."

"If they're not busy creating them," Walter said as he stepped behind the counter with Mrs. Hinkley's box of supplies.

"I heard that!" Gertie shouted from across the store.

"Put your earbuds back in," Walter said.

Mrs. Hinkley smiled and peered into the box. "Looks like you got everything, Walter."

"I'll put it on your tab, Belinda. Give me a call if you need any help with your windows. I've got Scooter on hurricane duty today."

"I'm hoping the new shutters take all the effort out of it, but I'll give you a call if I need help. Tell Scooter to stay safe out there. The wind is already starting to pick up."

"I'll let him know," Walter said.

"It was nice meeting you," I said.

"It was nice meeting you, too," Mrs. Hinkley said. "I'm glad to see Celia was wrong, as usual." She pointed to the box and Landon slid it off the counter, and followed his mother out of the store.

"Celia must really be losing ground," Gertie said as she pushed a box around the counter. "Belinda Hinkley is a hardcore Catholic."

Ida Belle hefted another box onto the counter. "Belinda's not bad. She's never bought into Celia's ravings. Never been a part of that silly God's Wives group of hers. Her husband was a commercial fisherman. Got killed in a boating accident back when Landon was about ten. Her whole life was devoted to that boy until he went to a group home in New Orleans three years ago. Then she took up gardening with a passion—vegetable gardening, not flowers. She has some of the biggest and sweetest tomatoes I've ever eaten."

Walter nodded. "If she'd grow more, I'd sell them in the store and we'd both retire."

"It's a shame the home closed," Gertie said. "Belinda said he was doing so well there, and the poor woman deserved some time to herself. But I guess you have to take care of your own."

"That is the truth." Walter looked into the boxes. "You sure you got everything? You might have missed the kitchen sink."

"We won't know if we need one of those until the storm is over," Gertie said. "And of course this isn't everything, but we'll supply our own cough syrup."

Walter began making a note of the supplies. "I'll put it on the church's tab. Same goes for you three as far as Scooter goes—if you need any help securing your homes, give me a call and I'll send him round."

"Are you coming to the church for the storm?" I asked Walter.

"Oh, well, I don't know that it's necessary," he said. "I'm pretty well fixed at my place. The ground's a little higher and I'm farther away from the bayou than you are."

"I was just thinking we might need help or something," I said.

Walter looked a tiny bit embarrassed and more than a little pleased. "Well, if you think I might be able to help, I suppose I could spend the night in a pew."

Gertie shook her head. "You're assuming the building won't explode if you walk inside. When is the last time you were in the church?"

Walter shrugged. "Whenever the last funeral was. Don't see any reason to go otherwise. Pastor Don comes in here once a week to buy groceries and he lays out his entire sermon for me then. No use hearing it twice. I don't need that much sleep."

Walter finished up the tab and said he'd have Scooter deliver the boxes to the church. We headed out of the store and hopped into my Jeep.

"What was that about?" Ida Belle asked.

"What?" I asked, trying to play stupid.

Ida Belle narrowed her eyes at me. "You know what. Playing Walter up as the big man so he'd come to the church."

Gertie leaned in between the seats. "Oh my God. You're playing matchmaker."

"I am not," I said, but it didn't sound very convincing.

According to Gertie, Walter had been in love with Ida Belle since he'd first set eyes on her when they were kids, and had even proposed a couple times, but Ida Belle remained staunch in her unmarried status. I got it, truly, I did. The thought of sharing a life, much less a bathroom, with the same man every day terrified me more than being lost in the desert with a leaky canteen, but I liked Walter, and he and Ida Belle weren't getting any younger. This might be the world's longest game of hard to get.

"Okay, fine," I said. "Maybe I am, a little, but it's not like I'm trying to push them up to the altar."

"Technically," Gertie said, "you did maneuver them both into church…"

"I was just repaying the favor."

"What favor?" Ida Belle asked.

"The one where you and Gertie kept pushing me and Carter together," I said.

Ida Belle frowned. "I don't push, especially when it comes to romantic entanglements, but you can't hold me accountable for pointing out what was already there. The attraction between the two of you is like flashing neon. Even a blind person could see it."

"True," Gertie said. "I had to order new sunglasses."

"That's because you needed a new prescription," Ida Belle said.

"I did not." Gertie flopped back in the seat and I grinned.

Ida Belle looked over at me and sighed. "I can't believe you played matchmaker. You're getting soft, Redding."

I laughed. "This may be the only time anyone ever says that to me."

Chapter Three

When the storm hit, it was a doozy. I'll admit to jumping straight up out of the pew when that first wall of wind hit the side of the church, but in my defense, it sounded like a freight train had just slammed into it. People started praying, dogs and children wailed, and cats yowled. Except for Merlin. He sat in the cat carrier Gertie had furnished, still giving me what Ida Belle had referred to as "the stink eye." He looked so angry, I was having second thoughts about going home with him after this was over. I had to sleep sometime.

Ally jumped up and went to talk to a couple of the waitresses at the café who were huddled in the choir loft. Walter and Carter got up and started walking the perimeter of the church, double-checking windows and doors to make sure they were secure. Ida Belle and Gertie sat slumped in their pews without so much as a twitch.

"Seriously?" I asked, staring down at them. "This doesn't bother you at all?"

"We're old," Ida Belle said.

"I'm not old," Gertie said. "I'm just fearless."

"You're so old you've forgotten to be scared," Ida Belle said.

The building shook as a second shock wave hit it. I looked up at the pulpit, which was swaying a bit from side to side. "You're sure there's nothing to be concerned about?"

"Look at it this way," Ida Belle said. "If there *was* something to worry about, what could you do?"

I stared at her for a moment. Hell, she was right.

I plopped down onto the pew next to her. "How long do these things usually last?"

"The worst of the storm is usually over in a couple hours," Gertie said. "We can have tornadoes for days, though. Tornadoes are sneaky. They don't announce their arrival all over the evening news like hurricanes do."

"Remember," Ida Belle said, "we're not getting hit straight-on. Otherwise, we'd be sitting in a casino somewhere in Oklahoma. Worst case, we'll probably have no power for a couple days. Best case, it will be back on tomorrow."

"There's no best case where the power stays on?" I asked.

Thunder boomed overhead and lightning struck the ground somewhere near the church. It was so loud, it made my ears ring. The lights blinked once, then went off, casting us into darkness. A couple seconds later, flashlights clicked on all over the church.

"Never mind my last question," I said. I turned on my flashlight and cast it over the church, spotting Carter and Walter hurrying for the front doors. "Where are they going in such a hurry?"

"To see if something's on fire or if someone needs help," Ida Belle said.

I shook my head. "Surely no one is crazy enough to be out in this?"

Ida Belle raised her eyebrows and looked over at Gertie.

"One time," Gertie said. "You go out into a hurricane one time and you never hear the end of it."

"You heard more about it from your insurance company than you did from me," Ida Belle said. "I was too busy laughing."

"Should I even ask?" I asked.

"Probably not," Ida Belle said, "but since you did, someone forgot they left their bass boat at the dock behind the butcher shop and decided to go retrieve it. She made it halfway down the driveway when Dorothy's oak tree got hit by lightning and fell right onto the trunk of Gertie's car, and since she always backs up with her hand on the gear shifter, she was startled into shifting the car from Reverse to Drive."

"I did not shift," Gertie argued. "The car did that itself."

"Sure it did," Ida Belle said. "Anyway, when the car shifted itself, it must have also given itself gas, because it launched forward, right into Dorothy's porch."

Gertie crossed her arms. "I never liked the tree or that porch."

I grinned. "What happened to the boat?"

Ida Belle waved a hand in dismissal. "That boat was probably halfway to Arkansas before she ever climbed in the car."

"I'm glad Scooter hauled my airboat up to the back of the house with his four-wheeler," I said. "I hadn't even thought about it going on tour."

"I will never let anything happen to that boat," Ida Belle said.

Her seriousness was just a bit scary. I was fairly certain Ida Belle loved my airboat as much as Walter loved Ida Belle. I heard banging behind me and turned to see Carter and Walter struggling to open the door. I jumped up from the pew and hurried to the back of the church, putting my shoulder on the door next to Walter's. "Try it again," I said.

Carter nodded. "One, two, three!"

On three, we shoved as hard as we could and the door flew open. The blast of wind hit me so hard, I had to take a step back to keep my balance. Raindrops felt like needles as they pelted my face. I threw one hand over my eyes and stepped forward to look outside with Walter and Carter. Walter pointed to a car across the street with smoke coming out of its hood. It was empty, and with the downpour, there was no risk of the fire spreading.

Carter nodded, and we grabbed the edge of the door to pull it shut. We were about two feet from done when one of those sonic blasts of wind descended on us and ripped the door from our grasp. I felt something thin and solid slap against my face and lowered my head, hoping that nothing heavier was blowing in the gale, like a telephone pole or a fire truck.

It seemed as if we struggled forever, but we finally got the door closed. A flurry of something that felt like leaves fluttered around us, dropping to the floor. I looked down and realized all of the leaves were rectangular, and frowned. I picked one up and shone my flashlight on it, then shoved it at Walter and Carter.

"It's money," I said. I flashed my light across the floor, illuminating the carpet of damp green hundred-dollar bills.

"What the hell?" Walter grabbed the hundred from my hand and held it right up to his face. "It's real. This is real."

"The nearest bank is a good twenty miles away," I said. "Could the storm carry money that far?"

Carter frowned. "Not likely."

"Also not likely that the nearest bank is twenty miles away," Walter said. "The nearest *commercial* bank might be that far, but I bet a lot of these old-timers have cash hidden all over this town."

"You think someone's retirement fund blew away in the storm?" I asked. "That would suck on all kinds of levels."

"Nothing we can do about it now," Carter said. "I'll get a trash can from one of the Sunday school rooms. Let's pick this up and hide it. If people catch sight of it, they'll be running out into the storm, swearing God was sending them money."

We gathered up the wet money and crammed it in a trash

can that Carter promptly stuck in a closet in one of the rooms off the back of the church. I shoved one of the bills into my pocket for closer inspection later on. The whole idea of money blowing around in a storm had my instincts on high alert. Something felt off. More off than normal Sinful oddities. And unfortunately, my "off meter" hadn't been wrong since I'd set foot in the town.

"I wonder how much more is out there," I said.

Carter shook his head. "I just hope no one else catches sight of it."

We made our way back to the pews, and I sank down in between Ida Belle and Gertie. I glanced back to make sure Carter and Walter weren't anywhere close before pulling the bill out and using my phone to illuminate it.

"There's money blowing around in the storm," I whispered. "A bunch of it flew in when that last blast hit."

Gertie grabbed my hand and pulled it over toward her face. "This is a hundred-dollar bill. You're telling me there's a hurricane of hunskis out there?"

"Don't get any ideas," Ida Belle said. "It could be a hurricane of gold bricks and it wouldn't be worth going out into that storm."

"Maybe not right now," Gertie said, "but bet your butt, I'm going to be the first out that door when the storm breaks. God's making it rain!"

A little girl, probably six, a couple pews in front of us turned around and nodded. "Of course God's making it rain, Ms. Gertie. Who else would it be?"

"Lower your voice," Ida Belle said, "or we'll have a stampede of idiots running outside."

I pulled the bill out of Gertie's hand and took a closer look at it. It looked legit and the paper felt right, but something about it still bothered me.

"You've got that look," Ida Belle said. "What's wrong?"

I shook my head. "Nothing that I can point to, but something doesn't feel right. I know that's a weak basis for concern…"

"I wouldn't say that," Ida Belle said. "I'd say someone with your abilities and training are attuned to things that aren't quite what they appear to be. If you think something's off, then I have no doubt something is."

"This is Sinful," Gertie said. "How would we know what's off and what's *off*, if you know what I mean?"

I shoved the bill back in my pocket. "She's right. Nothing in this town is what I'd consider normal, and I've been feeling nervous about the storm. That's not my norm, so my instincts are probably skewed."

Ida Belle nodded but didn't look convinced. I didn't blame her. I wasn't convinced either. My cell phone vibrated and I pulled it out of my jeans pocket, surprised I had any signal at all. I checked the display.

Harrison!

My CIA partner was the only person besides Director Morrow who knew where I was and how to reach me. His usual method of keeping me in the loop was email, cleverly disguised as discussions about weather, crops, and his dad. He never risked calling unless it was dire.

No way could I take the call here. I couldn't risk anyone overhearing me. I switched to text mode.

Can't answer at the moment. We're having a hurricane.

A couple seconds later, his reply came back.

Put the damn drink down and answer the phone.

I sighed.

Not a drink. A REAL hurricane. I'm holed up in a church with a bunch of people. Check the news.

I pressed Send and waited. I didn't have to wait long.

WTF Redding. Find a closet or confessional or something where you can talk.

My back tightened. Something was wrong. Harrison wouldn't insist unless that was the case. "It's Harrison," I told Ida Belle and Gertie. "He insists on talking to me now."

They cast worried glances at each other.

"On the right side of the church, in the door past the piano is a single restroom," Ida Belle said. "Use that. I don't know that you'll get enough signal to talk, but at least you won't be sharing the room with other women like the main bathroom."

I shoved my phone in my pocket and set off down the aisle for the restroom. It was located on a back corner of the church, and the outside walls almost hummed with the force of the wind hitting them. I locked myself in, pulled out my phone and dialed. It took three tries before I got a connection, and even then, I could barely hear Harrison.

"I can barely hear you," I said, "so talk loud, and fast. I don't know how long this connection will last."

"It sounds like you're in a wind tunnel."

"I am in a wind tunnel. It's a hurricane."

"You were serious about that?"

"Yes, and I'm serious about losing signal. Hurry up!"

"Your risk assessment just went from high to duck now."

I felt a chill run through me. "What happened?"

"Some counterfeit money turned up at a casino in New Orleans. It's almost a perfect match for the bills used to make the deal with Ahmad that we were working when you blew your cover."

My grip tightened so hard on the phone that my fingers started to throb. "You're sure?"

"Positive. The lab has done at least ten comparisons on the bills. The new ones are slightly cleaner, but the base workmanship is the same."

"What are the flaws?"

"The main one to look for is at the corner of the right eye. Remember how that section looked like it had been done in a hurry on the other bills? Well, it's much better now, but there's still a flaw at the edge."

I reached into my pocket and pulled out the hundred, then shone my flashlight on it, drawing it as close as possible to my face. Was that a break in the pattern in the corner of the eye? I needed a magnifying glass to be sure.

Or maybe I didn't. Maybe I already knew.

Ida Belle and Gertie looked up anxiously at me as I made my way back up the aisle and took a seat between them. Carter and Walter were checking a window at the back of the church and most everyone else had drifted off to sleep.

"What's wrong?" Ida Belle asked.

I told them what Harrison said.

Gertie's eyes widened. "You don't think the money in the storm is the same money, do you?"

"I can't see the bill well enough to be sure, but…"

"You had a bad feeling to begin with," Ida Belle said. "I'm sure you're right."

"But how can that be?" Gertie asked. "How could he have found you? I know you're not exactly low-profile in Sinful, but Sinful is not exactly high-profile around the world."

"I don't have any answers," I said. "Maybe it's a coincidence."

"You don't believe that for a minute," Ida Belle said.

"No, I really don't." I blew out a breath. "When we were tracking new buyers, there was one that we thought would receive shipment through the Gulf of Mexico. New Orleans is one of the logical places to conduct that kind of transaction. Boxes of cargo on large ships tend to go unnoticed when there are a lot of them."

"So if this new buyer received shipment through New Orleans," Ida Belle said, "that would explain how the counterfeit money got to the casino there. Everyone working the deal probably got counterfeit as payment and one or more of them headed to the casino."

"It makes sense," I said.

Ida Belle frowned. "I assume these suppliers don't tell Ahmad that they're paying him with counterfeit."

"Hardly. Ahmad has businesses all over the world that he uses to launder the money, so it might have taken a while to catch the first round. The work is good. I mean really good. You'd have to be an expert or have a machine to tell the difference. Even with the new security measures the counterfeit still passes a hard look by the naked eye."

"But it's not perfect," Gertie said.

"No. They're never perfect. Casinos are almost as good as banks for catching the fakes. Our lab is certain the bills found in New Orleans were a better rendition of the same bills Ahmad received for a previous sale."

"That explains why the bills are in New Orleans," Ida Belle said, "but why are they in Sinful?"

"I don't know," I said, but I wondered. Weeks ago, the ATF had been tracking an arms dealer through Sinful. The weapons were Middle Eastern in origin and fit Ahmad's offerings, but I couldn't be certain. And then there was a whole scarier thought to consider.

"What would happen if Ahmad found out the money was counterfeit?" Gertie asked.

Yeah. The scarier thought.

I didn't answer right away, and Ida Belle and Gertie looked at each other and then back at me. "You don't have any idea?" Gertie asked.

"No. I know exactly what he would do," I said. "He'd hunt them down and kill them."

Ida Belle narrowed her eyes at me. "Harrison said Ahmad recently fell off the grid, right? Surely he wouldn't personally execute such a plan?"

"Yes, he would. Ahmad is arrogant and more importantly, fearless. No one ever attempts to take over his business because he isn't afraid to make the kill himself. And they always suffer. His reputation keeps the jackals at bay. If he had an opportunity to send people a reminder, he would take it."

"So if the guns the ATF found running through Sinful originated with Ahmad," Ida Belle said, "and the same counterfeit money is here—"

"And Ahmad is missing," Gertie finished.

"Yeah," I said. "It means Ahmad could be on his way to Sinful."

Gertie bit her lower lip and gave Ida Belle a worried look. "Would Ahmad recognize you?" she asked. "I mean, you look completely different, right?"

"He'd recognize me," I said. "It's his business to know people, and he hates me. He won't forget. Not a single line or dip on my face. These extensions and a dress won't make a difference."

"Then you have to get out of here," Gertie said.

"At the moment, that's not an option, which is what I just spent a good sixty seconds trying to explain to Harrison."

"As soon as the storm is over," Ida Belle said, "we'll get you out of Sinful and somewhere safe. In the meantime, you keep a lower profile than dirt. As far as you know, Ahmad has no reason to suspect you're in Louisiana. Maybe he'll finish his killing and go on his merry way."

"Maybe," I said, but I had a feeling it wasn't going to be that simple.

JANA DELEON

Chapter Four

The blinding rain and hurricane winds ceased sometime in the middle of the night and switched to a gentle patter of rain. I dozed on and off on the pew, but never fell into a deep sleep. Ida Belle shifted a lot during the night, so I know she wasn't making much more of it than I was. Gertie, on the other hand, was dead asleep, splayed out on the pew like snoring roadkill. Really loud snoring roadkill. A couple people suggested stuffing her skein of wool into her mouth, but finally settled on shoving some of it in their ears. Carter and Walter sat at the back of the church near the doors, but I never saw either of them getting any shut-eye.

By the time the storm stopped raging, I was so ready to go home, I would have crawled if there were no other options. The only thing that kept me from going was Ida Belle pointing out that I had no idea if Sinful bayou was currently running through my living room, and that was something best investigated during daylight hours. The thought of swamp creatures inhabiting my downstairs was enough to put me back in the pew.

When the first ray of sunshine peeked through a crack in the storm shutters, a cheer went up in the church. Everyone was exhausted and tired and praying that the damage was minimal. People started heading for the door, stir-crazy and anxious to get outside. Carter pushed open the doors and a line of people trailed out of the church, dragging garbage bags and ice chests of personal items.

And then we heard the first yell.

"Money! The streets are full of money!"

People who were slogging along suddenly gained the energy of fifty Olympic athletes. They bolted for the doors, almost knocking Carter off the steps in their pursuit. Gertie leaped up from the pew and ran with the crowd. "Wait for me!"

I looked over at Ida Belle. "She was there when we discussed how there was a good chance the money was counterfeit, right?"

"She was as 'there' as she ever is."

"Never mind. We better go check."

We headed out of the church and stopped on the steps next to Carter and Walter, who were surveying the situation on Main Street with helpless expressions. A frantic mob of people ran like rats on acid through the streets, some of them practically tackling the bills on the ground before another person could scoop them up. Gertie was right in the middle of the fray, stuffing hundreds into the front of her shirt as fast as she could nab them.

"Should we do something?" I asked.

Ida Belle and Walter simply shook their heads. Carter looked conflicted. "You and my mom keep reminding me I'm on medical leave," he said.

I rolled my eyes. "Please. You're not going to try to pass off your concern for your mother's and my feelings at this late date. If you had any desire to jump into that fray, you would have already done it. Maybe you should just fire your weapon or something."

"I'm not sure what they're doing is illegal," he said.

"Only on the first Tuesday in September," Ida Belle said.

"There you go," Carter said, apparently committed to staying right where he was.

I didn't bother to ask for an explanation. Sinful had all sorts of strange laws, all dating back to when Columbus discovered the earth wasn't flat. For all I knew, the first Tuesday in September was the only day designated as illegal to roll around in money.

"The cavalry has arrived," I said and pointed to Sheriff Lee, who was headed down the street on his horse. Technically, I suppose he was the former Sheriff Lee given that Celia had fired him and replaced him with her criminal cousin who was now behind bars and awaiting trial, but apparently that hadn't stripped the ancient swamp cowboy of his sense of duty. If only his ability, and that of his equally ancient horse, matched his devotion to his job, things might go better than they usually did.

Sheriff Lee pulled out a gun and I waited for him to lower it at someone and set off the "Bang" flag that was inside, but this time, he wasn't playing around. He pointed the gun in the air and pulled the trigger. A second later, a flare shot out of the gun and into the sky, stopping people in their tracks.

"I can pull out the real one if needed," Sheriff Lee shouted.

Deputy Breaux, who was serious about his job but young and inexperienced, ran down the street toward the sheriff, waving his arms. "Don't shoot!"

Gertie stepped in front of the horse and glared up at Sheriff Lee. "What the heck are you doing, you old coot?"

Gertie's shouting must have registered with the elderly horse, who hadn't even twitched when the flare shot off, because he lowered his head to look at her…but the lowering didn't stop. The bills that Gertie had been stuffing into her top were spilling over the neckline and the sheriff's horse had zeroed in on the green stuff, which he apparently took for a tasty horse-type snack. He stuck his nose right into Gertie's shirt and snagged a mouthful of the bills.

Gertie screamed and tried to shove his head out of her

cleavage. "Your horse is molesting me! I'm pressing charges."

The horse, realizing that the wad of paper in his mouth wasn't a tasty snack after all, threw his head up and snorted, spitting the slimy bills and a good wad of horse snot onto Gertie. Deputy Breaux ran up and grabbed the horse's reins to lead him away from Gertie, who was standing stock still, eyes closed and hundred-dollar bills stuck to her face.

She reached up to grab the bills, but instead of flinging them away as I would have, she clenched them in her hand. She looked over at us, and I imagine we were all wearing the same look of disgust and disbelief. "I have Febreze," she said.

"Well, at least the horse snorting cleared the street," I pointed out, not certain what to think about a group of people who were more afraid of horse snot than Sheriff Lee firing a loaded weapon.

"There's more back here!" A voice sounded from somewhere in the woods behind the Catholic church.

"Shut up, you moron!" another voice shouted.

The few people lingering around on the sidewalk took off like a shot around the church. Gertie cast a wistful glance at the runners, then sighed. "I'm not going to run in the forest in these stockings. They attract ticks."

I stared. Why the heck were ticks attracted to stockings? And if she knew that, why in the world was she wearing them? The mind boggled.

"My Jeep made it through the storm," I said. Ida Belle, Gertie, Ally, and I had all taken my Jeep into town to wait out the storm, figuring it would be a better choice to get around in the aftermath. "Should we make the rounds?"

Ida Belle and Gertie nodded. "There won't be power," Ida Belle said, "but at least we can get an idea of what repairs might be needed. The sooner you get your supplies order in, the better."

"Be careful," Carter said. "I'm going to drive around and make sure no one is stranded in the storm. Let me know how everything looks."

"Wait for me." Ally ran down the church steps. "I hope the storm didn't blow my new construction away." Ally's kitchen had been the victim of an arsonist and was being rebuilt. In the meantime, she was staying with me and I was reaping the benefits of living with a baker extraordinaire. Unfortunately, my taste buds weren't the only part of me reaping. My butt and thighs needed that kitchen to be complete, or the only thing I was going to fit in was clothes with elastic waists.

"What about Merlin?" I asked.

"Leave him here for now," Ida Belle said. "He's safe in the church, and you can come back and get him once you know where you'll be staying tonight."

"Cool." We climbed in the Jeep and I drove to Ally's house first. She hopped out of the back and jumped onto the sidewalk.

"Show off," Gertie mumbled.

"Go ahead and take off," Ally said. "It will take me a bit to go through everything. Are you staying at the church again tonight?"

"No," I said. "Assuming the bayou isn't running through my living room, I'm staying home." I'd spent three nights in a ditch and one memorable occasion tucked partially under a camel's stomach. I could deal with no electricity. No electricity was child's play.

"If it's not habitable," Ida Belle said, "you guys can bunk with Gertie or me."

"Thanks," Ally said and headed off for her house.

"Do either of you have a microscope?" I asked, figuring it was a long shot, but in Sinful, you never knew.

"Of course," Ida Belle said. "I've been working on my own gunpowder mixture. I like to get a good look at it."

Gertie shrugged. "I just use mine to check my fingernail polish."

I headed for Ida Belle's house, figuring she'd know exactly where to find her microscope. Gertie was far less organized. I'd found a box of tissues in her refrigerator last week and a Weed eater in her pantry. She'd been looking for the Weed eater for at least the three days before.

We made a quick run through Ida Belle's house and gave it a pass. A couple of trees had lost limbs that would need to be hauled off, but other than a good debris cleanup, everything was otherwise undamaged. Ida Belle's microscope was in the middle of her dining table along with several canisters containing black powder.

"Why can't you just keep flour like everyone else?" Gertie asked.

"Because I don't want to be like everyone else," Ida Belle said.

I glanced out the window at the sunshine peeking through the clouds. "Let's take this outside. I need more light." We headed into the backyard, where I righted the picnic table and put the microscope on it.

"You want one of mine?" Gertie asked, pulling a hundred from her bra.

"This one will do," I said, and pulled the bill out of my pocket.

I stuck it under the microscope and moved it over until I was focused on the corner of the eye. The markers Harrison had told me to look for were all there.

"Damn," I said and straightened up.

"It's a match," Ida Belle said, not even bothering to ask.

I nodded. Somehow, I'd known it would be, but I was still hoping I was wrong—that my instincts were all off-kilter because of the storm and had gotten mixed up.

"What do we do now?" Gertie asked.

The knot in my stomach slowly dissipated and I smiled.

What do *we* do now?

That one simple word made all the difference. I wasn't alone. In five weeks, I had made friends who cared about me enough to get in the way of the deadliest arms dealer the world had seen in at least a decade.

"You have to lie low," Ida Belle said. "And that's going to be more difficult because of the storm."

"Crap," Gertie said. "I hadn't even thought of that, but she's right. Every hotel between here and Mobile will be booked from people evacuating. But there's other places to hide. Not as comfortable and won't have room service, but Ahmad wouldn't find you."

"I'm not hiding out on Number Two," I said. The swamp island got its name because of the stench of the mud that made up most of it. It was a favorite for local fishermen, but I was fairly certain their nostrils had gone numb and they could no longer smell it.

"Number Two is known by too many locals anyway," Ida Belle said. "Someone might see you and mention it in passing, then it's all over."

"There's another problem to consider," I said. "How am I supposed to explain my sudden desire for lonely places to Carter?"

Ida Belle frowned. "I hadn't thought that far, but that's a problem. If the hurricane hadn't hit, we could have passed off a trip to New Orleans and gotten you out long enough to get our bearings, but now, I don't know."

"You have to tell him," Gertie said.

Ida Belle looked at her, then at me, and sighed. "I'm afraid she's right. I know in the beginning you felt you were protecting people by not telling them the truth, and I agree, to an extent. But now, I think you're not telling Carter because you're afraid to."

I felt my chest constrict. Ida Belle was always direct, but she didn't usually tackle the emotional side of things. Unfortunately, she'd exposed the biggest lie I'd been telling myself. I was afraid to tell Carter the truth. My feelings for him were unlike anything I'd ever experienced, and selfishly, I didn't want it to end. Carter was an honorable man. When he found out I'd been lying to him, he was going to be angry and hurt and disappointed. When he found out why I had been lying to him, and who and what I really was, he'd be even angrier, and maybe even disgusted. Sure, he'd served in the military and had probably known a sniper or two, but it was a completely different thing to wrap your mind around your girlfriend's being an assassin.

"What if he doesn't want to be around me anymore?" I asked.

Gertie put her hand on my arm and squeezed. "Honey, this day was always going to come. Don't you think it's better to get it over with than let it linger until the end of summer? At some point, you're going to leave here. That's always been the case."

"I know," I said. "I guess I never figured things would go this far. I'm not exactly girlfriend material."

"Maybe you weren't before," Gertie said, "but you've changed since you've been here. Can't you see that?"

"I guess so." It was more than a guess. I knew I'd changed, but I still wasn't comfortable with it. Admitting I'd changed meant thinking about whether or not I was the person I was supposed to be. Finally assessing how much my mother's death and father's neglect and professional reputation had shaped the decisions I'd made.

It meant that I had to figure out who I was, because I'd never really known.

Ida Belle's phone buzzed and she looked down at the display and frowned.

"It's Marie," Ida Belle said. "She said something is wrong at Celia's house and to get over there."

"Of course something is wrong at Celia's house," Gertie said. "Celia lives there."

"Marie's not an alarmist," Ida Belle said. "We better go see what's up."

As we made our way back through the house, Ida Belle tried to call Marie, but the call wouldn't go through. We jumped into my Jeep and made the couple blocks' drive in less than a minute.

Marie was standing in Celia's front lawn, next to a man sitting on the ground, his hands clutching his head. "That's Norman Phillips," Gertie said. "He's a friend of Celia's."

I screeched to a stop and we hurried over. Norman didn't even look up when we approached, but it didn't take a medic to see that he wasn't well.

Five feet eleven inches. A hundred ninety pounds. Weak liver. White as a corpse and shaking like a Chihuahua. A Chihuahua would probably be a bigger threat.

"What happened?" Ida Belle asked.

Marie shook her head. "He must have stopped to check on Celia's house for her. I heard someone scream and when I looked out the front window, he was running out of the house and fell down on the front lawn. He hasn't said a word. Just sits here shaking."

"He's in shock," I said. "Did you go inside the house?"

Marie's eyes widened. "No way. I sent a 911 text. The

paramedics are on the way and hopefully some form of law enforcement, but with the storm…"

"I'll go look," I said.

"Maybe you shouldn't," Marie said. "Norman isn't the toughest man in the world, but he's no pansy. I don't have any idea what could have done this to him."

"Is Celia still at the church?" I asked.

"I saw her standing in the doorway when we pulled off of Main Street," Gertie said.

"I'll be right back." I headed for the front door and Ida Belle hurried beside me. I didn't bother to tell her not to come. Ida Belle was me in forty years, and I was as stubborn as they came. We walked up onto the porch and I slipped through the partially open door. The living room looked fine, so we headed toward the back of the house. It took a single step into the kitchen to know what had Norman working on the fetal position.

What was left of Max Arceneaux lay facedown on the kitchen floor directly in front of Celia's sink.

"Shotgun," Ida Belle said. "Two blasts at least."

I nodded. "Shot point-blank. The cabinet kept him from launching backward."

"Let's get out of here," Ida Belle said. "You didn't touch anything, did you?"

"I never do. Professional habit."

"Good. Because the last thing you need right now is to get caught up in a mess like this."

"And boy is this going to be a mess," I said. "Walter said Celia went into the store and bought shotgun shells right after her run-in with Max at the café."

Ida Belle whistled. "I hope there was a church full of people with eyes on Celia the entire night."

We slipped out the front door and headed down the sidewalk. "Surely," I said, "Celia wouldn't have sneaked away and killed Max. How would she even know he'd be here? And why was he here?"

"No. She wouldn't have. If he'd broken in and threatened her, maybe, but despite all the things Celia is capable of, I don't think murder is one of them."

"But that won't stop other people from thinking so," I said.

"Especially everyone who heard or heard about the exchange at the café."

Gertie looked up at us as we approached. Sirens sounded close by, which was good. Norman hadn't improved one bit since we'd left. In fact, his breathing had started to increase and I was afraid he'd have a panic attack before the paramedics could get him oxygen. Ida Belle shook her head at Gertie and she looked over at Marie, who bit her lower lip. We couldn't say anything with Norman there, but they both knew that whatever was inside that house was bad.

An ambulance pulled up to the curb and two men jumped out and rushed over to Norman. Right behind them, an SUV screeched to a stop and Celia burst out of the passenger side door, waving her hands. "What the heck is going on? What did you do to Norman?" She glared at me.

"She didn't do anything to him," Ida Belle said. "Marie found him this way."

Celia smirked. "Like I believe that. Anytime she's around, there's trouble."

"Oh, there's trouble," I said, "but it has nothing to do with me. You might want to save being belligerent for after the cops get here."

Celia cast a worried glance at her house, then back at us. "What happened to my house?"

The paramedics helped Norman up and headed for the ambulance. Ida Belle waited until they were out of earshot before replying. "Your house is a crime scene."

Celia threw her hands in the air. "What the hell are you talking about, you old fool? Hurricane damage is not a crime."

"Murder is," Ida Belle said.

Chapter Five

Gertie sucked in a breath and Marie's hand flew up to cover her mouth, and it took me a second to remember that they didn't know what Ida Belle and I had found inside any more than Celia did.

Celia put her hands on her hips and glared. "I don't know what kind of stunt you're trying to pull this time, but I won't fall for it." She whirled around and stomped off toward her house.

"Don't go in there!" Ida Belle yelled. "For once, will you trust me?"

Celia glanced back at Ida Belle with a hold-your-breath-and-wait look but never slowed her pace.

"Stubborn, foolish bitch," Ida Belle said.

"Should I stop her?" I asked.

"No. Let her go in and take a look. Serves her right. Not like she's going to disturb the crime scene. Her prints are all over the house anyway."

"Who's dead?" Gertie asked.

"Max," Ida Belle said.

Gertie's eyes widened and Marie gasped as the blood rushed from her face.

"You're sure it was murder?" Gertie asked.

I nodded. "Shotgun blasts to the chest at close range. Probably two. Maybe more. He fell forward so it's hard to tell without turning him over."

Gertie understood exactly what I described and her face wrinkled up for a moment. Marie simply sank onto the lawn, her hands clutched together.

A loud shriek rang from inside the house and a couple seconds later, Celia came running out the front door, tripped on the doormat, and face-planted on her porch. Gertie hurried over and leaned over to check on her. "She's breathing. Just passed out, I think." She headed back down the walkway. "The paramedics can see to her when they're done with Norman. We told her not to go in there."

"Yeah, well, the situation is even worse than it looks," I said and repeated what Walter had told me the day before at the store.

"Celia couldn't have shot him," Marie said immediately.

Gertie nodded. "She doesn't have the chops. Look at her now—passed out like a drunk at New Year's. She wouldn't have made it out of the house after shooting him."

"What we think is not going to matter," Ida Belle said. "Unless eyes were on Celia at the time Max was shot, she's suspect number one. The front door is broken, but with the hurricane, there's no way to prove it was forced versus the damage is because of the storm."

"I tried to get her to replace that old door when I did mine," Marie said. "But of course, she wasn't about to do it since it wasn't her idea."

"Of course," Ida Belle said.

One of the paramedics walked up. "Do you know what happened to him?"

I gave the young man a brief description of the scene in the kitchen. His eyes widened and I saw his throat move as he swallowed. "Thanks, ma'am." He hurried away, casting a worried glance back at the house. He was probably terrified that they'd be asked to go in and get the body.

"Here come the police," Gertie said. "Such as they are."

Carter's truck pulled up and he and Deputy Breaux climbed out and headed our way.

"What happened?" Carter asked.

Ida Belle gave him a rundown. Carter's expression darkened. Deputy Breaux, who I thought would be upset, seemed to take the news the way he did any other report of a crime, like drunk and disorderly. Then I remember that he probably heard and saw a lot worse during hunting season and it put things back into perspective.

"Why is Celia passed out on the porch?" Deputy Breaux asked, glancing over at Celia's heaving chest. "Was she attacked as well?"

"Only by her own stupidity," Ida Belle said. "We told her not to look."

"Ah." Deputy Breaux nodded. "The paramedics can handle that one then. We're not required to handle stupid."

"Are you kidding me?" I said. "That's all you handle in this town."

"Touché," Gertie said

"We have to document the scene," Carter said.

"You're still on medical leave," I reminded him.

"It's an emergency situation. I'm reinstating myself. Deputy Breaux can't walk the scene alone, and I don't have the authority to deputize any of you."

Gertie's eyes widened. "Oh, that would be great. Who has the authority?"

"The sheriff," Carter said.

"But we don't have a sheriff," Gertie said. "Not technically."

"Then no one," Carter said. "So don't bother getting ideas."

I smiled. The last thing Sinful needed was Gertie with a badge. She did enough damage with her handbag of tricks without a license to arrest people. And Sheriff Lee was probably just irritated enough that at this point, if he had the authority, he would hand her over a shiny piece of metal. I glanced at Ida Belle, who was looking at Gertie and frowning. Probably the same thoughts were running through her mind.

"Let's get this over with," Carter said and headed for the porch, Deputy Breaux trailing behind him.

As they stepped onto the porch, Celia bolted upright and grabbed Carter's leg. "I want that woman arrested," she said and pointed to me.

"For what?" Carter asked.

"For that," Celia said and pointed inside her house.

Carter's jaw set in a hard line and I could tell he'd finally reached his politeness breaking point with Celia.

"Here we go," Ida Belle gleefully whispered.

"Here's the way the law works," Carter said, "since it's clear you aren't smart enough to know. First, there's an investigation where we gather evidence. Once we have evidence, we arrest people. I don't care if you're mayor of the universe. You still can't direct me to arrest someone without evidence. So either shut up and let me do my job correctly or get in there and clean your own damned kitchen."

"Ooooohhhhh, bull's-eye," Gertie said and clapped as Carter stepped over Celia and entered the house. Deputy Breaux hesitated a moment before skirting Celia's legs and hurrying inside.

Celia glared at their retreating backs for a couple of seconds, then turned her hateful look on us. "Don't think you're getting away with this."

"With standing on your front lawn?" I asked. "Last time I

checked, it wasn't illegal. I'm sure you can get that changed but until then, I'll just wait here and enjoy the show."

Celia rose to her feet and stomped down the porch. "You think this is entertaining? A man is dead and you don't even care."

"And I'm supposed to believe you do," I said. "I heard you threaten him yesterday in the café, and I know that you went across the street and bought shotgun shells right after that little encounter. One of us is in a heap of shit over Max's murder, but I guarantee you that it's not me."

Celia gasped and the color drained from her face. "I didn't...I never," she sputtered.

"Then you don't have anything to worry about, do you?" I smiled. "After all, no one in Sinful would ever railroad an innocent person for their own personal pleasure."

"Another bull's-eye," Gertie said.

Celia shot a nasty look at Gertie, then shoved her to the side and stalked across the lawn and climbed back in the SUV. The vehicle squealed away from the curb and I watched as it turned the corner.

"Hey," I asked, "who was driving the SUV?"

"Freda Williams, one of Celia's lackeys," Ida Belle said.

"She never got out of the vehicle," I said. "Not even when Celia passed out on the porch."

"She's an idiot, and a coward," Ida Belle said, "and she's afraid of Gertie."

"Why is she afraid of Gertie?" I asked, glancing over at Gertie, who chose that moment to study her shoes.

After several seconds of uncomfortable silence, Gertie finally threw her arms in the air. "You shoot someone accidentally one time and they hold a grudge forever," she said.

I stared. "You shot her?"

"My knitting got wrapped around my pistol," Gertie said. "It was an accident."

"The pistol she forgot to put the safety on," Ida Belle said.

"That bullet barely touched her," Gertie argued. "It hit her butt and there's a lot of acreage there. She didn't even need a bandage, but the biddy wailed so much they gave her a little one."

"Ma'am," one of the paramedics interrupted. "We're going to take this gentleman to the hospital. Would one of you like to come along, or is there someone you can call for him?"

"I'll come," Marie said. "I can call his daughter on the way. She's in New Orleans, so it would take her a while to get here, assuming she can get away after the storm."

"Great," the paramedic said and headed back to the ambulance.

"I'll call you when I'm back home," Marie said. "Find out everything you can. This was next door to my house. That doesn't sit well with me." She gave us a nod and headed toward the ambulance.

"You don't think Marie's in any danger, do you?" Gertie asked.

"No," Ida Belle said. "Timing worked out for her. She wasn't home to see the shooter. If she'd been home at the time of the murder, she would have heard the shots and would have looked outside. But since she was at the church with us, then no."

"Do you think the killer knew that?" Gertie asked.

"My guess is yes," I said. "If Max came here for something, he did it when he knew the house would be empty. It would have been easy enough for someone to check the two churches and see who was there."

Ida Belle nodded. "I don't think anyone on this street stayed put. Several have relatives in north Louisiana and head that direction when a storm moves in. Others were at the churches."

"That's good," Gertie said, looking relieved. "Marie doesn't need any more trouble."

"Agreed," Ida Belle said, "but until they establish time of death, I'm afraid she might have some. Celia is angry and afraid right now, but once she calms down, my guess is she'll shift her attention from Fortune and accuse Marie of the murder."

"Why in the world would she do that?" Gertie asked.

"To claim that Marie did it to implicate Celia in a crime in order to get the mayor position."

I whistled. "She would do it, too. Let's hope the time of death is narrow enough and far enough back that Marie was still perched in the church in front of a bunch of witnesses."

"Your lips to God's ears," Gertie said.

We stood in silence, waiting on Carter and Deputy Breaux to emerge. They were probably only inside fifteen minutes or so, but it felt like forever, especially once the mosquitoes moved in. I slapped another on my arm and almost wept with relief when they came out the front door.

"Can you please take our statements now," I asked, "before we're carried away by the mosquitoes?"

Carter nodded, then looked over at Deputy Breaux. "Take their statements at the sheriff's department. The generator should give you enough power for some lights and a computer. I'll wait for the coroner and seal the house." He glanced around. "Where did Celia go?"

"She hightailed it out of here," Ida Belle said, "after telling Fortune she wasn't going to get away with it."

Carter rolled his eyes.

"Then Fortune reminded her that she'd threatened Max in the café and went directly to the General Store to buy shotgun shells, and that shut her up and sent her packing."

"She did what?" Carter looked at me.

I nodded. "That's what Walter told me."

"Damn it." He looked at Deputy Breaux again. "Find my uncle and take his statement as well, and then find Celia and instruct her that she can't enter her house without a police escort and she needs to remain in town."

Deputy Breaux's eyes widened and I knew he was thinking of all the horrible things that might happen when he confronted Celia with that set of instructions. I felt sorry for him. Gertie patted his arm. "I'll make you a nice Bundt cake," she said. "That and some Sinful Ladies Cough Syrup should help take the edge off."

Deputy Breaux looked at Gertie. "Do I get the cough syrup and cake before I talk to her or after?"

Gertie dug a bottle of cough syrup out of her purse and handed it to Deputy Breaux. "I can handle that part now. The cake will have to wait until I have electricity. But I promise it will be worth the wait."

Deputy Breaux didn't look convinced that the cake was an equal trade for having to talk to Celia, but he seemed happy with the cough syrup part of the deal. "Then I guess we better get going," he said.

We headed for my Jeep and followed Deputy Breaux back into town.

"Celia is going to have kittens when Deputy Breaux gets a hold of her," I said.

Gertie nodded. "I started praying as soon as I got in the Jeep."

"Praying for what exactly?" I asked, curious as to how she pitched such a thing to God.

"Well," Gertie said, "I started off with praying for strength for Deputy Breaux so that he doesn't run away like a chicken. Then I prayed that Celia doesn't have a weapon on her besides her mouth."

"That's a good enough one," Ida Belle threw in.

"Then," Gertie continued, "I asked him to make Celia do something stupid so that Deputy Breaux would have to arrest her."

"Why in the world would you want her arrested?" Ida Belle asked. "That's just punishing Deputy Breaux."

"I know," Gertie said, "but the thought of Celia spending a night in the slammer, with no electricity, makes me all gleeful."

I grinned. It sorta made me gleeful too.

I could tell Deputy Breaux would have liked our statements to take longer, but as we didn't really know anything, there wasn't much to state. Forty-five minutes of reprieve was all the young deputy got before he had to approach the task that he did not want to mention. Gertie gave him a hug, which probably frightened him even more, and then we left.

"Let's try this again, shall we?" I said.

We had just pulled up in front of Ida Belle's house when my phone rang. "It's Ally."

"What the heck is wrong with Aunt Celia?" Ally asked. "She called me all ranting about you and the café and Max. She sounded absolutely crazy. And I mean in the real way, not in the usual Aunt Celia way."

Crap. There was no love lost between Ally and Celia, but given that Celia was her aunt, Ally needed to know what was going on.

I covered my cell phone and looked over at Ida Belle. "She says Celia's gone crazy. I can't tell her all this on the phone."

"Go pick Ally up," Ida Belle said. "Gertie and I will check on my house and then head over to hers. If your place isn't habitable, give me a call and we'll put you two up at whichever one of our places fared the best."

"I'll pick you up in a minute," I said to Ally, and disconnected the call. Ida Belle and Gertie climbed out and I gave them a wave as I drove away.

Ally was standing on the curb in front of her house when I pulled up. "How is everything with your house?" I asked.

"Good," Ally said, looking enthusiastic. "There was no visible damage. The bayou crept up in the backyard a good ways, so I imagine some things in the storage shed are ruined. I put my lawn equipment in the garage when I heard the storm was headed this way, so nothing major lost."

"That's good. Fingers crossed that my house did as well. If not, we can bunk with Ida Belle or Gertie."

Other than some random debris in the lawn, my house looked good from the front. No storm shutters missing. No bald spots on the roof. No random swamp creatures wandering about. As long as no one could drive a boat into my kitchen, we might be in good shape. I pushed open the front door and headed straight down the hallway for the kitchen. So far, so good. The tile was dry and showed no signs of having served as temporary bayou real estate.

I looked out the kitchen window and let out a sigh of relief. The bayou was halfway up the backyard, but it was still a good thirty feet from the house. "We don't have to build an ark," I said.

"Good," Ally replied, "because I don't build things unless I can use power tools. I put together a bookcase one time with a regular screwdriver and couldn't use my right arm for two days."

"Let's make sure the windows upstairs are intact," I said. "If so, then I'll fire up the generator to make sure it works, and I'm good to stay here tonight if you are."

"I don't care if the generator doesn't work. As long as my flashlight works long enough to get me upstairs and into a real bed, I'm all for it. Those pews are not comfortable for sleeping."

"They're not all that comfortable for sitting, either," I said.

"If Pastor Don is preaching, you're still trying to sleep."

"Good point." I stepped onto the upstairs landing. "You take the right and I'll take the left."

I headed into my bedroom and gave it a look. The windows looked sound with no leaking, and nothing strange had climbed up the bathroom plumbing. My bathtub was still full of water, so everything was ready for Operation Hurricane Roughing It. I did a quick check of the other bedroom and bath, then headed back downstairs to the kitchen with Ally.

"How long will the stuff stay good in the refrigerator?" I asked.

"In this heat, only a couple of days. You can hook the generator up to it for a couple hours here and there to draw that out. We probably need to eat as much of it as we can. Lucky for our thighs that you're a minimalist when it comes to domestic pursuits."

"Or unlucky, depending on how long the power is off."

"Don't worry. Every time there's a bad storm, practically the entire town ends up at Gertie's house for a barbecue. The woman packs meat away like she's preparing for the Apocalypse."

"What happens at the café?" Between Ally, Gertie, and Francine's Café, I made out pretty well as far as eating went. I didn't want to imagine a Sinful where all of them were out of food at the same time.

"Francine spent a ton of money on generators, and she gets

priority on gas to run them. Even the sheriff's department gave up a slot to push Francine up the gasoline list."

"As well they should." I snagged a couple of sodas from the refrigerator, opening it only a crack and closing it as quickly as possible, then slid them onto the table and took a seat. "I have something I need to tell you."

Ally frowned and sat across from me. "You never start a conversation like that. It must be bad."

"It is. Not for me for a change, but it's about Celia...and Max."

"Nothing about Aunt Celia and Max could be good."

"Yeah, but this goes beyond the usual. Max is dead."

Ally sucked in a breath and her eyes widened. "The storm?"

"I'm afraid not, unless hurricanes can fire shotguns."

She paled a little. "Oh my God. I never liked him that much and I liked him even less after that scene at the café. I know Celia's a bitch, but he went out of his way to be cruel. Still, that doesn't mean I wanted someone to kill him."

"Of course not. And if it makes you feel any better, I didn't like the way he handled the café either."

Ally nodded, then gasped. "It was...Aunt Celia didn't..."

"No. At least, I don't think so, and neither do Ida Belle and Gertie, but he was found in her kitchen, and she bought shotgun shells from Walter right after she left the café."

"Oh no! That's not good."

"It may be fine. If time of death was during the storm, then Celia should have been visible to plenty of people over at the church. She'll have a dozen or more ironclad alibis."

"And if time of death is sketchy?"

"She'll have to cross that bridge if it comes, but I wouldn't worry about it. You know good and well that Carter is not going to focus on the easy answer and ignore all the facts. He's known

Celia all his life. I don't think he likes her for this."

Ally bit her lower lip. "I hope not. Aunt Celia and I have our problems, but she's still family. And even though she can be mean as a snake, I just don't see her shooting Uncle Max in cold blood."

"I don't either, but he was in her house, and that looks odd. Max was inside Celia's house for a reason. If she didn't ask him there, then I don't know why he went. Do you?"

Ally slowly shook her head. "Aunt Celia got rid of everything that belonged to him. I helped her haul a bunch of his clothes to one of those mission churches out in the swamp. She sold his guns and all of his fishing tackle. His boat was the only thing of value that she hung on to, but someone stole it and sank it."

I nodded. I was well aware of the stealing and sinking of Max's boat, as I'd been on board when both happened. "But you said she never used it. I wonder why she kept it?"

"Ha. She said if he ever showed up again, she was going to set it on fire. She always complained about the amount of time he spent on the boat."

"I'm going to hazard a guess that it wasn't because he loved the boat, or he would have come back for it a long time ago."

"Of course not," Ally said. "He was just using it to get away from Aunt Celia."

"And once he left town, he didn't need it any longer. Still though. It had to have been worth a good bit of money. You have to wonder what he's been doing all this time."

"If we knew that, we might be able to figure out who wanted to kill him."

I shook my head. "I'm not figuring anything out. Carter has read me the riot act more than once over getting involved in police stuff, and besides, the last place I need to insert myself is anywhere Celia is. She's just looking for a reason to send me to jail."

That's what I said, anyway, but I knew that as soon as I got a chance, I'd be poking not just my nose but my entire body into the middle of that mess. I had no particular reason why. Not yet. But so far, my visit to Sinful had been predictable in only one area—if there was a crime committed, I was right in the fat middle of it.

Chapter Six

Once the house had received the go-ahead for rough living quarters, I headed back into town and picked up Merlin. When I opened the cat carrier on the kitchen floor, he stalked out and stared at me before demanding to be let out the back door. If looks could kill, he would have melted me on the spot. I had a tiny bit of concern about sleeping that night. He'd pulled a drive-by on my forehead once, and those razor-sharp claws had drawn blood.

Ally and I had just popped the top off of a couple bottles of beer when I heard a knock at my front door. It was pushing toward evening and I'd already talked to Carter, who had put himself back on duty and was planning on staying at the sheriff's department that night just in case anyone was stranded and managed to get an emergency call out.

I swung the door open and was surprised to see Gertie and Ida Belle standing there. "We thought we'd have a slumber party," Gertie said as I waved them inside.

"Really?" Nothing about her tone said lighthearted fun.

Ally walked into the living room and gave them a wave.

"My generator is on the blink," Ida Belle said. "I figured since yours was working, it was a better idea to bring my gas over here and pour it into one that wasn't going to crap out in the middle of the night."

"And I wasn't about to sit home all by myself and let you

guys have all the fun," Gertie said.

"Cool," I said, although I didn't buy it for a minute. Nothing ever crapped out on Ida Belle. As soon as that storm started forming, she'd probably gone outside, fired up that generator, then done a complete clean and lube or whatever the heck you did to make sure they ran properly.

Fortunately, Ally wasn't nearly as suspicious as I was. "That's a great idea," she said. "We were just about to have a beer and leftover German chocolate cake if you're interested. We're waiting until it cools off a bit more, then we're going to fire up the grill."

"Thank God," Gertie said and trailed off down the hall after Ally. "I have at least fifty pounds of hamburger meat in the trunk of my car."

"What's really going on?" I asked as soon as they were out of earshot.

Ida Belle gave me an innocent look. "What do you mean?"

"Your generator probably runs better than Junior's stock car."

"Nice NASCAR reference. You're really catching on to this Southern thing. And you're right. My generator is top notch, but your situation warranted company."

"How's that?"

"We didn't want you here alone with the possibility of Ahmad breathing down your neck. You need backup, and unfortunately, not only is Ally not in on the real situation, she wouldn't be good backup even if she was. In fact, she makes the situation even more volatile by her presence alone."

"Crap." Ida Belle was right. Even if Ally knew the truth, she wasn't trained to handle Ahmad and his men. Quite frankly, neither were Ida Belle and Gertie, but they were light years ahead of my friend, who knew more about baking than shooting.

"I don't really think anything will happen," Ida Belle said. "But I wouldn't feel right knowing you two were here alone."

"Maybe we should move to your house. If Ahmad is looking for the new person in town as a means to locate me, then this is the first house they'd check."

"Not necessarily. If strangers start asking about new arrivals in town, Sinful people won't think of you right off the bat. They all think you're Marge's niece, not someone new. And besides, the description wouldn't match at all."

"Maybe not the shaved head, but tall, fit, age-appropriate, and mouth all fit."

Ida Belle frowned. "True."

"It's too late to do something tonight. The plan is already in place. We'll stay here tonight and reassess in the morning. Hopefully, Harrison will have some more information soon. He's supposed to text as soon as he knows anything, then I can call when I'm clear to."

Ida Belle started to say something, but stopped when Gertie and Ally came back into the living room.

"Gertie says she has enough ground meat in her car to feed half of Sinful," Ally said. "We're going to haul it out and make hamburgers tonight, and I'll mix up some for meat loaf. It's good for us that Fortune doesn't keep much in her refrigerator besides beer. With Ida Belle's gas, we should be able to keep it fresh for several days."

"I guess the upside is that I won't need my iron pill," Ida Belle said. "At least this time it's beef. Last time, Gertie had more chicken than KFC. I couldn't eat chicken or eggs for almost a year."

Ally grinned and headed outside. Gertie lagged behind. "Did you tell her the plan?" Gertie asked.

"I hadn't gotten that far yet," Ida Belle said.

The word "plan" had taken on a whole new connotation since I'd met Gertie and Ida Belle, usually an illegal one. "What plan?"

"Well, first, we figured we'd cook up the burgers and you could take some to the sheriff's department for Carter and work your feminine wiles on him to get the scoop on Max," Gertie said.

"Then I reminded Gertie," Ida Belle said, "that she'd just put you and 'feminine wiles' in the same sentence."

"Right," Gertie said, "but as Carter is a man, I figured you could distract him simply by standing there."

"Given that he's a man," I said, "isn't he just as likely to be distracted by the burger?"

Ida Belle looked over at Gertie, who threw her hands in the air. "I know. I know. You already said that. But if Fortune is there, then it's double the distraction, and last time I checked, a hamburger couldn't talk someone into staying put if we need it."

"Why, exactly, do we need Carter to stay put?" I asked.

"So that Ida Belle and I can read Carter's notes on Max, of course."

I shook my head. "I'm flattered by your faith in me, but even if I was standing in Carter's office, wearing hamburgers like a bikini, I don't think he'd miss you two going through his paperwork."

Gertie perked up. "A bikini burger. I could work with that."

Ida Belle glanced at Gertie, her expression a mixture of "what the heck" and "Good God, woman."

"Actually," Ida Belle said, "Carter will probably be up front since it's only him and Deputy Breaux on duty. Marie is staying at the church again tonight with some people whose houses aren't habitable. She'll let us know when Deputy Breaux goes out for a patrol, and then we'll swoop in. Then you only have to keep

Carter up front eating while we visit Carter's office by way of the ladies' room excuse."

I'd visited Carter's office by way of the ladies' room once and lost a perfectly good pair of tennis shoes in the process. "And what if his notes are up front with him?"

"Then you'll have to get him back into his office somehow," Gertie said.

"And I'm supposed to do that how?"

"That hamburger bikini idea had some merit," Gertie said.

Ida Belle waved a hand at her. "If the notes are up front, then one of us will create a distraction that gets him away from the front and you can read the notes."

"This is the weakest plan ever," I said. "And that's saying a lot."

Ally banged into the screen door and Gertie hurried over to open it. "Sorry about that," she said to Ally. "We got caught up talking about ground beef recipes."

Ally raised an eyebrow, while clutching at least fifteen packs of ground meat. "Fortune was discussing recipes?"

"She was discussing what she'd like to eat," Gertie said.

Ally grinned. "That I can believe." She headed down the hall.

"We'll work on the finer details," Gertie said, "but that's the basic plan. We better go get that meat before it spoils."

She didn't have to ask me twice. Gertie's car was one of our main means of transportation when we were investigating…yeah, that's it. "Investigating" sounded a lot better than "breaking the law." Anyway, given her refusal to buy new glasses and a host of other issues, I didn't want her driving my Jeep, and the three of us couldn't fit on Ida Belle's motorcycle. So the Caddy was often our only choice, and if it smelled like a ten-day-old crime scene, I was going to start walking.

We headed outside and I stopped short at the trunk of the Cadillac. Gertie hadn't been kidding. The entire thing was stuffed with packages of ground meat. I picked up one of the packages and looked at the handwritten label.

"Did you run over a brontosaurus?" I asked, remembering a previous unfortunate cow incident that I'd heard about.

"No, smarty," Gertie said. "If you must know, a friend of mine retired from farming and liquidated everything before he moved to a condo in Florida."

I shook my head. "If we manage to eat all of this, I could take the starring role in the next Iron Man film. I probably won't even need a costume."

"If we eat all this," Ida Belle said, "the only role we'll be starring in is the toilet paper one."

I grabbed an armful of packages and headed for the house. According to Marie, quite a few people couldn't return home yet and roads weren't clear enough to leave town. A batch of hamburgers delivered to the churches would probably be a welcome sight. I just hoped Walter had some buns left in the store.

I dumped the load on the kitchen table next to the stack that Ally had carried in. She had already taken the three big mixing bowls out of the cabinets and was gathering the seasoning.

"I figured we could take some of this to the churches once they're cooked," I said.

"That's a great idea," Ally said. "Sandwiches can get old."

"I need to call Walter and see if he has any buns left."

"I've got buns," Gertie said as she lurched into the kitchen with an armful of meat.

Ida Belle stepped in behind her. "She's referring to the kind you eat. Not the kind you sit on."

Gertie gave her the finger, and the packages of meat exploded from her grasp and scattered across the kitchen floor.

Ida Belle shook her head. "Why didn't you just stick out your tongue? We really have to work on your efficiency skills."

"I'm retired," Gertie said as she picked up the meat. "How efficient do I need to be?"

"How many buns do you have?" I asked, interrupting their argument.

"A bunch," Gertie said. "I had Walter order them in when I saw the storm coming."

Ida Belle dumped her meat on the counter and turned to stare at Gertie. "Is that what's in those giant trash bags in your backseat? What if that storm had turned and headed to Florida?"

"Then I would have hosted a party at the park," Gertie said. "Like people here would turn down free food."

"Is there more meat?" I asked.

Ida Belle nodded. "I'm pretty sure there's a black hole in the bottom of Gertie's trunk and meat is coming through it from another planet. We've hardly made a dent."

I was just about to head out for another load when I got a text message. It was Harrison.

Call me as soon as you are able. Have information.

I glanced over at Ida Belle and inclined my head toward Ally. Ida Belle gave me a slight nod, and I headed outside to call Harrison. Cell phone service wasn't all that strong, but the call went through.

"Is the storm over?" Harrison asked.

"Yes, but there's no power and some of the homes are damaged."

"Can you get out of town?"

I clenched the phone. Harrison was careful, which is why I liked partnering with him. He didn't have the kind of showboat tendencies that got agents killed, but he wasn't an alarmist.

"I don't think the roads are clear yet," I said. "What did you find out?"

"Two of Ahmad's men were spotted at a casino in New Orleans. A field agent made them at a craps table. They passed off some of the fake hundreds."

I blew out a breath. I'd been hoping for the best, but I'd gotten the absolute worst. "You're sure it's the same money?" I asked, even though I already knew the answer. Harrison would have made them check the money five times over to be sure.

"The field agent got with the manager and got the bills. They match the ones that were passed off before. I don't have to tell you how serious this is. Ahmad missing and his men turning up in New Orleans with the counterfeit money…they're too close."

I thought about the hundred-dollar bill in my pocket. "You have no idea."

"What do you mean?"

I filled Harrison in on the windstorm of hundreds that had hit Sinful. I'd barely finished when he started a string of cursing. "You've got to get out of there. I don't care if you leave by boat or on foot. Hell, I can send a helicopter."

"Because *that* wouldn't be noticeable. And where would I go? New Orleans is clearly out, and that's the nearest big city. The airport and bus station are out. If Ahmad has any idea that I'm here, he'll have men watching those places."

"Well, you can't stay put, either. You're a sitting duck in that town with only one way out. And despite the fact that we worked carefully on your cover image, you've managed to stick out like a sore thumb with all the crap you've wound up in the middle of."

I started to argue, but didn't have a good comeback. The truth was, he was right. I had done a horrible job of disappearing into small-town America. I'd been in the fat middle of every major crime that had happened in Sinful since I'd arrived and managed to complicate things even more by dating a deputy. It was like I'd never received a day of training in my life. And while I didn't regret any of the things I'd done, I could totally understand why Harrison was so frustrated.

And then an idea began to form…it was a long shot, but hadn't my entire trip to Louisiana been just that?

"You're thinking about this all wrong," I said.

"I don't think so."

"You're trying to get me to safety, but safety is an illusion until Ahmad is dead. If he's discovered the counterfeit money, and the presence of his men suggests that he has, then this is a prime opportunity to take him down."

"No way. It's too dangerous."

"How is it any more dangerous than doing it overseas? I have an advantage here. We have no reason to think that Ahmad knows I'm here. We suspected he had new buyers in the area before I ever blew cover. He won't be expecting me. We can take him down—make this entire mess go away forever."

"Do you even hear yourself? Mounting an operation would take weeks. We have days at the most. And with that storm that just blew through, law enforcement availability will be at an all-time low."

"So fly them in. Call one of your buddies at the FBI and tell him this is his chance to put a promotion in the bag. Buy him season tickets to whatever sports team he's into. Hell, buy him a hooker. Just make it happen."

Harrison went silent, and I knew he was running through all the possibilities.

"I'm not really a librarian," I said quietly. "Let me do my job."

He sighed. "Damn it, Fortune. Let me talk to Morrow and see what he thinks."

"But you're with me on this?"

"God help me, but yeah, I am. I'll text you once I've talked to Morrow."

I disconnected and shoved the phone back into my pocket. Ida Belle must have been watching from the living room, because she pushed the door open and came outside, under the guise of retrieving the hamburger buns. She pulled a garbage bag from the backseat and handed it to me.

"So what's the news?" she asked.

I filled her in on what Harrison had told me and my request for backup for a takedown. Her expression shifted from concerned to downright worried.

"Do you think that's a good idea?" she asked.

Her tone was inquisitive and completely nonjudgmental, which pleased me to no end. Rather than take the line of the worried friend, which I knew was also the case, she'd chosen instead to be a soldier.

"Honestly, I don't know," I said.

"Then maybe you shouldn't do anything."

I set the trash bag down and leaned against the car. "It's not that I don't trust myself to do the job. I absolutely do, and no one wants this over with more than I do."

"But?"

"But I have everyone here to consider. I'm talking about bringing the devil to Louisiana so that I can exorcise him."

Ida Belle frowned and nodded. "You're worried someone will get caught in the cross fire."

Yeah. That was exactly what I was worried about. Not so much the regular citizens who were going about their business, completely unaware of what was happening right under their noses. But I knew that despite my best efforts, I wouldn't be able to keep Gertie and Ida Belle from wanting to help. The only way to keep them out of it would be to lie and avoid, and although I was normally an expert at both, the idea of doing it to them upset me more than I thought it would.

And then there was Carter. I knew I needed to tell him, but was now the right time? He'd totally go all white knight trying to protect me, and the last person I wanted caught up in this was him. Not that I underestimated his ability. Carter would make a fine CIA operative, but his feelings for me might cloud his judgment, just as my feelings for him were doing now.

Tell him or not tell him. That was the question.

If only I had the answer.

Ally tossed another hamburger patty into a foil tray. "If I never smell ground meat again as long as I live, it will be too soon."

I looked around the kitchen. At least thirty more burgers and ten trays of meat loaf remained to be cooked, and there were still another five packs of ground meat to go. Even Merlin, who'd initially been delighted with a raw meat snack, had gotten stuffed and headed outside to collapse in a patch of sunlight. "We look like we're catering for cavemen."

Ida Belle came in the back door with another stack of cooked patties. "This makes seventy. Ally, if you'll cover up some of those trays, we can haul some of this to the church. Fortune, why don't you fix up a tray for Carter and Deputy Breaux. I'm sure they'd appreciate a hunk of red meat since they're working the night shift."

"I completely forgot about that," Ally said as she pulled a box of tinfoil from my pantry. "I wonder if they ever found Aunt

Celia."

One of the hospital aides had gotten off shift about the time Marie finished up at the hospital and had given her a lift and a dose of gossip on the way back to Sinful. The aide had overheard Norman trying to call Celia on his cell phone. He'd apparently moved from catatonic to merely scared half to death and regained the ability to talk.

The aide had only overheard one side of the conversation, but apparently Celia had decided to hide out and Norman was less than happy about the decision. I didn't blame him. He went to do the woman a favor, saw the most horrible thing he'd probably ever seen in his life, and instead of sticking around to hold his hand while he relived it all with police, Celia had totally dropped off the map.

"Who knows if they found her," I said and placed a stack of buns in a tray alongside eight hamburger patties. "I don't get that woman. She's just making things worse on herself."

"She's trying to regroup," Ida Belle said. "She finally ran into a situation that's over her head. And that useless bunch of biddies that follow her around aren't going to be any help. If the truth was known, some of them probably think she did it."

"If they didn't before, they do now," Ally said.

Ida Belle nodded. "Celia's an old fool, but I think there's more to it this time. This time, I think she might actually be scared."

Ally turned around to look at Ida Belle, her expression thoughtful. "I'd never really thought about it, but you may be right. I'm so used to Aunt Celia the Ball-Breaker. It's hard to switch gears and put her in the victim role."

"I wouldn't go that far," I said. "As soon as she gets over being scared and indignant, she'll launch a campaign to get Marie arrested for Max's murder."

Ally sighed. "You're right. I won't bother switching gears. I probably wouldn't have been there very long anyway."

I pulled tinfoil over my tray of food and secured it. Ally sat two more containers on the kitchen table as Gertie walked in with another stack of cooked patties. "This is the last one I have outside," she said.

Ally nodded and assessed the remaining uncooked meat. "I think we can fit the rest in the refrigerator, including the ones I haven't made yet. We probably shouldn't cook any more today."

"Yay," Gertie said and flopped into a chair. "I'm starting to feel a little charbroiled myself."

Ally slipped a bottled water out of the refrigerator and passed it to Gertie. "You've been standing over that grill for hours. I'm surprised you haven't melted."

"There's a decent breeze—thank God, or the mosquitoes would have been a bigger problem than the heat." Gertie lifted the bottled water and wiped it across her forehead. "I don't even feel like eating after all of that."

"Good," Ida Belle said. "You can help us deliver these to the church and the sheriff's department while Ally finishes up with the last of the ground meat. Maybe you'll be hungry after you move around a bit."

"Probably," Gertie said, perking up a bit.

I checked my watch. Marie had reported to Gertie that Deputy Breaux was doing rounds every hour and a half. That meant he should be leaving the sheriff's department in the next ten minutes or so, assuming he kept to schedule.

Ally stacked two more trays on the table. "Do you think this will be enough?"

"How many does that leave us here?" I asked. I had no problem with being generous, but after all that work, no way was I eating a bologna sandwich while half of Sinful feasted on burgers.

"There's twelve in this tray," Ally said. "And then, of course, everything that we haven't cooked."

"I think twelve will tide us over until tomorrow," I said. I slid Gertie's car keys over to her and grabbed a stack of trays. "Let's get this show on the road."

We piled everything into the backseat of Gertie's Cadillac and headed for downtown. We were halfway there when Gertie's cell phone went off.

"Crap," Gertie said. "It's Marie. Deputy Breaux just left on patrol."

"He's early," Ida Belle said. "How long have the patrols taken?"

"About thirty minutes," Gertie said. "We need to hurry."

Chapter Seven

Gertie slammed her foot down on the gas pedal and the car lurched forward. I scrambled to grab the stacks of trays before they fell onto the floorboard. "A little warning next time," I said.

"Sorry," Gertie said. "Sharp turn!"

I leaned over the trays as if I were protecting a small child from a bear attack as Gertie wheeled the car around the corner.

"Slow down, you old fool," Ida Belle yelled. "This won't work if we don't have hamburgers to bring to the sheriff's department."

Gertie let up on the gas a tiny bit and made the final turn onto Main Street. I relinquished my protective position and looked between the seats and down the street. A handful of people were picking up debris on the street and sidewalks and waved as we pulled up. I recognized a couple of them from the night before at the church and figured they must be some of the people who couldn't return home yet.

"Looks like they've organized a bit of a cleanup," Ida Belle said.

"They probably got tired of sitting on those uncomfortable pews," I said.

"Pastor Don got back in town today," Gertie said. "He started preaching about three hours ago and hasn't let up since."

"I hope he stops before tonight," I said, "or they'll be sleeping outside with the mosquitoes."

Ida Belle nodded. "Let's sneak these in and hope he doesn't see us."

"I've got a better idea," Gertie said, "and it will save us some time." She climbed out of the car and whistled. "We've got burgers here. Come grab a tray and take them to the churches."

Everyone stopped what they were doing and hurried for the car. I passed out hamburger trays like a dealer at a blackjack table, and a couple minutes later, everything was gone except the tray for the sheriff's department.

"Time?" I asked as I grabbed the last tray and we hurried for the sheriff's department.

"Fifteen minutes since he left on patrol," Gertie said.

"Then we've got fifteen minutes, give or take, to get this done," Ida Belle said.

"I still say the feminine wiles thing would work faster," Gertie said.

"Not if Fortune's the one executing," Ida Belle said.

I suppose I could have been insulted, but there wasn't really any point given that she was right. "Just get the information and don't get caught."

"Stop worrying," Gertie said. "We've got this."

I wish I felt as confident as Gertie sounded, but I had some experience with executing plans with Ida Belle and Gertie. The only thing consistent is that they never went the way we intended.

I pushed open the door to the sheriff's department and stepped inside. Carter was sitting at the front desk, as predicted, and gave me a weary smile. "Hard day?" I asked.

He lifted up a stack of paper about an inch high. "Four missing persons reports. Three vandalism reports. Five burglaries, and eighteen reports of missing cats."

"That's a lot of missing cats," I said, glad that Ida Belle and

Gertie had insisted on caging Merlin and taking him to church with us. He may be pissed now, but he'd thank me later. Or not. He was a cat.

Carter laughed. "I see where your priorities lie."

"Oh," I said, feeling a bit dismayed at my callousness.

"Stop ribbing her," Ida Belle said. "You know good and well those four people aren't missing. I bet I can tell you who they are." She rattled off the names of four men.

Carter nodded. "Got every one of them. You win the big prize."

"I don't get it," I said.

"Those four are drinking buddies," Gertie said. "They also happen to be married to four of the most difficult women in Sinful, excluding Celia of course. Every time there's a big storm, they pretend they're going round to help people and then 'accidentally' get caught in the storm."

"So where are they really?"

"Probably sitting at a motel up the highway," Gertie said, "drinking beer and watching all the HBO they want in peace in quiet. They'll turn up tomorrow with some story about being stranded while helping a fisherman or a tourist or saving a family of squirrels, and everyone will be happy."

I tried to fathom choosing a life that required a hurricane moving in for me to be happy but couldn't make the leap. Besides, we had work to do.

"I came bearing gifts," I said and put the tray on top of the stack of paperwork.

He lifted the end of it and sniffed. "That smells delicious." He looked at Gertie. "Did you run over a cow again?"

Gertie threw her hands in the air. "Why can't I just be a meat hoarder? Why does everyone assume I killed something?" She pointed at Ida Belle. "Don't answer that."

Carter grinned. "If you guys don't mind, I'm going to start on one of these right now."

"Feel free," I said. "We've been working on them all afternoon and kinda got enough by smell. But then, we had chips and dip and apple pie to snack on while we were working."

"You're killing me, Smalls," Carter said.

"I don't get it," I said.

"*Sandlot* reference," Gertie said and clapped. "As soon as the power is back on, we'll watch it. I love that movie."

Carter plopped a hamburger patty on a bun. While his gaze was directed down at the food, I poked Gertie in the ribs. We were running out of time.

"I need to use your restroom," Gertie said. "Do you have water jugs in there?"

Carter took a big bite of the burger and nodded.

Gertie set off down the hall. Ida Belle hesitated a couple seconds. "I better go too. Last time Gertie had to pour water into a toilet tank, there was an incident." She took off after Gertie, Carter and I staring after them.

"I don't even want to know," I said. "Especially since they're bunking with me tonight."

"Did they have damage?" he asked.

"No. Ida Belle just figured we'd consolidate gas use on one generator and at least get to run a fan inside."

He nodded. "I wish I knew how long power would be out. I'd kill for a fan right now."

I pulled my T-shirt from my chest, where it was clinging. "I can imagine. This building is super hot compared to my house."

"No north-south windows. I can't get a good draw through here, and then with the humidity from the rain, it's awful."

"If it doesn't come on in a day or two, I imagine we'll relocate until it does. Assuming we can find a hotel, of course."

"You might have to go a ways north, but bet your butt I would if I wasn't stuck here. Roads should be completely clear by tomorrow."

My cell phone buzzed and I pulled it out of my pocket, figuring it was Harrison. It wasn't. It was Ida Belle.

Max's info isn't on his desk. Must be up front.

Crap. I couldn't exactly start sorting through his paperwork with him sitting there.

Create a diversion. Then I'll check the desk.

"Is something wrong?" he asked.

"What? Oh, no. It's Ally," I lied. "She's finishing making up the last of the hamburger patties and wants to know if she should heat up some pastries for dessert."

"That sounds wonderful," Carter said.

"Sorry. If I'd known she had frozen pastries, I would have brought some with me. So I hear Celia pulled a disappearing act."

Carter sighed. "Where did you hear that?"

"It's all over town."

"Of course it is."

"So are you looking for her?"

"I don't have to look for her," Carter said. "She's hiding at her friend Freda's house, and since Freda didn't want to be accused of harboring a felon, she called and ratted Celia out."

"With friends like those…"

"I should go arrest her on principle, but I don't want to listen to her mouth all night. I figure Freda deserves it more."

"Definitely." I glanced down the hall, wondering what the hell was taking them so long. Deputy Breaux would be back any minute and we hadn't found out anything. I was just about to ask him for a roll of paper towels or something equally inane when I heard a yelp from the back of the building. Then Ida Belle came running back up front.

"Gertie's locked in the bathroom," Ida Belle said, "and the door is jammed."

"What?" Carter rose from the desk. "I just replaced that hardware a couple months ago."

"Come take a look before she panics."

Gertie started yelling and banging on the door. "I've got the claustrophobia. I can't breathe."

"Too late," Ida Belle said and took off down the hall again.

Carter dropped his burger and set off after Ida Belle. I ran around the desk and started shuffling files as quickly as I could. Burglary, assault, gaming violation…Max Arceneaux!

I opened the file and started reading. The cause of death was two shotgun blasts, as expected, but given the weather and lack of air-conditioning, the medical examiner hadn't been able to narrow time of death very well. His best guess was a window from yesterday evening until around 1 a.m. I flipped the page over and saw a copy of a driver's license that had Max's picture on it but a different name.

Thomas Johnson.

I made a mental note of the address and license number and flipped that page over. The last thing in the file was a plastic bag with money in it. My pulse quickened. It was hundred-dollar bills. I leaned over to get a better look, but without a magnifying glass, I couldn't be certain the bills were fakes.

I shoved the file back where I'd found it and was about to hop up when I saw another file peeking out from the stack. It was labeled simply "Money." I pulled it out and was just about to start reading when I heard commotion down the hall.

"I'm fading out!" Gertie yelled. "Tell my mother I love her."

"Your mother died thirty years ago," Ida Belle yelled back.

"Pull on the damned door."

"Back up, Gertie," Carter said. "I'm breaking it down."

I cringed and scanned the file.

I heard a loud crash. Then Gertie scream. Then Carter cursing.

I shoved the file back where I'd gotten it from and went running down the hall. Ida Belle was standing outside the now-open door to the restroom, shaking her head.

"What happened?" I asked.

"Gertie," Ida Belle said and pointed.

I took one hesitant step forward and peered into the restroom. Gertie was splayed out on the floor against the back wall, pinned into place by the toilet, which had taken leave of its normal spot and was lying on its side, water dripping out of the tank. Carter was pushing himself up from the top of the toilet and glared down at Gertie.

"Why didn't you tell me the door had come loose?" he asked.

"It was too late," Gertie said. "I barely had time to get out of the way. Get this thing off of me."

"I ought to leave you there for a couple hours," Carter said. "Give all of Sinful a break from your brand of terror."

"I take it the door came loose before Carter tackled it?" I asked.

Ida Belle leaned toward me and whispered, "It was never stuck. Gertie was pushing against it."

I closed my eyes and shook my head, a clear visual of what had happened running through my mind. "So the door flew open and Carter stumbled in and tackled the toilet."

"Pretty much."

I watched as Carter pulled the toilet off Gertie and helped her up. "Do you have any idea of the debt we owe to that man for the crap we put him through?" I asked.

"Let's just hope he never collects."

Carter headed back to the door, his expression a mixture of frustration and exhaustion. He checked the lock and the doorjamb, then closed and opened the door several times. "It's working fine," he said.

"Oh," Gertie said, looking guilty. "Maybe I was pushing instead of pulling."

Carter threw his hands in the air and headed down the hall, apparently too mad to even speak.

"I hope those burgers are spectacular," I said.

"This is all your fault," Gertie said. "And I was improvising. If you could do the whole girlie thing, that stunt with the door wouldn't have been necessary."

"How did this become my fault?" I asked, and looked over at Ida Belle. "Shouldn't this be your fault for letting her move forward with that lame idea?"

Ida Belle shrugged. "Did you find the paperwork?"

"Yes."

"Then we got what we came for," Ida Belle said. "I'm more of a results sort of scorekeeper."

"Figures."

I headed for the front of the building. Carter was already back at the desk, finishing up the rest of his burger. "I'm sorry about all the drama," I said. "Hopefully, the food makes up for a little of it."

"We'll be going to the General Store to pee until I can get a plumber out here—which won't be anytime soon—but the burger was good," he admitted. "Still, next time, everyone goes to the bathroom before they get here. Or you use it with the door open."

"Or simply in your right mind," I said, and smiled at Gertie, who gave me the finger.

"We best get out of the man's hair," Ida Belle said. "We've interrupted him enough and he's got a stack of work to take care of."

As I reached for the door, Deputy Breaux walked in, a good ten minutes later than usual. Carter gave him a dirty look. "*Now* you come back," Carter said.

Deputy Breaux looked confused. "What did I do?"

I patted his arm. "I'm sure you'll hear all about it. Have a hamburger. It will soften the blow."

We hurried out of the sheriff's department and hopped in Gertie's car.

"Darn, I wish I could take a shower," Gertie said. "I've got toilet water on me."

"Gross," I said. "I'm putting a trash bag over the kitchen chair, and burning the sheets after you leave."

"I'd make her sleep on the back porch," Ida Belle said.

"I'm never doing that again," Gertie said. "I dug splinters out of my butt for a week. Do you know how hard it is to see your own butt?"

I looked at Ida Belle. "You made her sleep on the porch?"

Ida Belle nodded. "During the last big storm. There was this unfortunate incident with a skunk."

"I thought it was Sara Jo's cat," Gertie grumbled.

"No rescue operations," I said, "and we're spraying you with Febreze."

"Please tell me it was worth the trouble," Ida Belle said.

I nodded and filled them in on what I'd read about Max. "He had some hundred-dollar bills on him, but I couldn't tell if they were the fake ones."

Ida Belle frowned. "I wonder how long they were blowing around in the wind?"

"Impossible to know," I said, "which is unfortunate, because if he picked them up off the street, we might be able to narrow down time of death."

"Maybe," Ida Belle said, her expression thoughtful.

"I found another file," I said. "It was one for the money. Carter's going to have it tested for authenticity as soon as he can get some to the lab."

"Interesting that Carter made the same leap you did," Ida Belle said.

"He's smart," I said, "and has good instincts."

"But yet," Gertie said, "you've managed to escape detection, despite all the compromising positions he's caught you in."

"That makes sense, though," Ida Belle said. "Carter is attracted to Fortune, which filters his view of her, and the leap from librarian to CIA operative is a huge one."

"Maybe," Gertie said, "but it's a leap he needs to make. Now that we know the counterfeit money used to pay Ahmad is in Sinful, and you're planning a coup with your partner at the CIA, you have to tell him the truth."

"I don't know if I'll get to stage a coup," I said. "Harrison has to talk to Director Morrow. I can't make a move without his approval. I need the backup he could arrange."

Ida Belle shook her head. "You're only delaying the inevitable. Today, tomorrow, next week. It's going to come out, and better he hears it from you than you disappear again and we have to tell him why."

"I'm not telling him," Gertie said. "I've inflicted enough horror on the man. No way am I taking that one on."

I sighed. "If Morrow gives the go-ahead for the coup, I promise I will tell him. Just maybe not until it's over."

"Because if he knew beforehand, he'd want to be in the

middle of it," Gertie said. "I get that."

"I don't," Ida Belle said. "You *will* need his help. Carter knows this town and the swamp surrounding it as well as any of the old fishermen and more importantly, he's qualified to help."

"Qualified, yes," I said, "but he doesn't have clearance. This is an international investigation. Without clearance from the CIA and, if they agree to assist, the FBI, telling Carter what's going on before it happens would be a federal crime."

Ida Belle and Gertie exchanged glances.

"But you're going to tell us, right?" Gertie asked.

"Sure," I said, "but that's different. No one will suspect that I've told you anything."

I tried to sound nonchalant with my answer, but I saw Ida Belle's eyes narrow slightly. She knew I was lying. No way was I telling them details of the takedown. I didn't want anyone I cared about caught in the cross fire.

And the only way to ensure that was to go it alone.

Chapter Eight

It was close to 3 a.m. when I finally got a text from Harrison.

Call me.

That was it. No "I have a plan," "we're on," or anything else. Except for the fact that it was the middle of the night, there was no other indication that my request for a setup might have been granted. A simple "Hell no!" would have taken a lot less time.

Without the AC running, the house was eerily quiet. And since the rain had stopped, there was nothing to mask me talking. I couldn't risk being overheard by anyone, so I crept downstairs and slipped out the back door. I looked up at the back of the house, but it was so dark, I couldn't tell if the bedroom windows were open. Not wanting to risk it, I stepped out into the yard, turned on my penlight, and started walking as I dialed. Two bars of service. I hoped it was enough.

"Please tell me he went for it," I said as soon as Harrison answered.

"He took some convincing, but ultimately he agreed with you—this may be our best chance to get Ahmad. We're operating on American soil, and we have an advantage, assuming he doesn't know you're already in position."

I climbed onto my picnic table and sat on the top. "I don't think his men are here for me. If they knew where I was, I'd already be dead."

"Agreed. And Morrow thought so as well, but we both agree that the only choices were to take Ahmad down now or relocate you. As much trouble as you've had with this gig, we thought it would be less hassle to take down Ahmad than saddle you with another identity."

There was a slightly teasing tone in Harrison's voice, but he wasn't wrong. I hadn't exactly blended in Sinful as I was supposed to. I could blame Ida Belle and Gertie, but the reality is, I simply couldn't pretend to be a helpless female if someone was in danger. I was trained for action, not to stand around waiting for a rescue.

"So what's the plan?" I asked.

"Morrow contacted his buddy at the FBI. He explained the situation except the part where you're on location. He simply said he had someone in a position to provide local intel. He thought it best to leave your name totally out of it."

"Good." If the CIA was compromised, the FBI could be as well. Someone with Ahmad's means could easily afford to have an agent or two in their pockets. "So what's the play?"

"Ahmad is still off-grid, but we know he's in contact with someone in the organization because the business end of things is still moving."

"And no way did Ahmad turn over decision-making to someone else."

"Exactly. Our guys in New Orleans have been sitting on Ahmad's men, waiting to see what move they made. So far, they appear to be trying to track Jamison's organization back to its primary location."

"Makes sense." Conrad Jamison was the buyer in New Orleans we suspected had a deal in place with Ahmad. If Ahmad had discovered the counterfeit bills, then he'd want to track

Jamison to his home in order to deal with the problem. And since this kind of business screwup couldn't be fixed with a gift card or a free dessert, Ahmad's men wouldn't want Jamison's crew to know they were coming. Not until it was too late.

"The FBI agents Morrow contacted have a line on Jamison's business interests in New Orleans. They think they can get us an address to work with, but they don't think Jamison is doing the deals directly. They think that end of Jamison's interests is being handled by someone else and so far, they haven't been able to figure out who."

"But they know where Jamison's home base is?" We'd been looking for that bit of information ourselves, but Jamison had proved to be a wily and somewhat eccentric target. He favored living in RVs and on shrimp boats and camping in the woods to staying put inside the same four walls. And if he subbed out business interests to different factions, then he automatically added another layer of insulation to himself, not to mention left someone else to take the fall if things went south.

"They don't think it's his home base, but it's an address that can be traced back to Jamison if Ahmad's men decide to check. It may be all we can get with our time constraints."

"If Jamison is connected to the location, that will be enough for Ahmad's men. How are you going to feed them the address?"

"The two agents watching them are going to break cover and pretend to work for Jamison. They're going to say they just found out about the counterfeit money and want nothing to do with it. They're going to give up the address in exchange for safe passage out of New Orleans."

"That's risky. I assume the information exchange will happen in a public place?"

"The airport. We'll have a charter waiting for them. They'll go through security, then we'll have people in place to get them to the FBO where the jet will be."

Everything sounded solid so far. The agents on site had a viable and reasonably safe escape route, and if the address could be tracked back to Jamison, then Ahmad should have enough to make a move. "And we'll be in place waiting for the strike at the provided location. What if Jamison is there?"

"Even better," Harrison said. "Two birds and all. The FBI has been waiting for enough ammo to take down Jamison. With what we gave them, they might have enough to start making a case."

"When will the agents give the information?"

"They'll make contact tomorrow and schedule the airport meeting for the next day."

"What's my role?"

"For now, see if you can figure out the Sinful connection. That money got loose in that storm somehow."

"You think Jamison has someone here."

"I think Jamison has people all over southern Louisiana."

"So I flush out the connection."

"Yeah, but be careful. Jamison's man could be someone you already know. And if Ahmad finds out there was money in Sinful, he'll send men there."

Crap. "I think that ship has already sailed." I told him about the file Carter had and his intent to run a check on the funds. "If Ahmad's got intel in the labs, he'll hear about it."

There was dead silence for several seconds and I pulled my phone away from my ear to make sure I hadn't gotten disconnected. Finally, Harrison said, "Do I even want to know what you were doing looking through the deputy's desk?"

"Getting intel, of course."

"And you just strolled in, asked to read his case files, and he handed them over with a smile?"

"No. I brought him hamburgers. Then my friends distracted him so I could read the files."

"The two old ladies?"

"Yep."

"Be careful, Fortune. The fewer people know about this the better. I know you said they can be trusted, but at this point, it's not about trust. It's about ability."

"I know. There's no way I can keep them out of things in Sinful. They were running this place from behind the curtain long before I showed up, but I have no intention of telling them about the plan. I don't want them in danger. Is there anything else?"

"That's all I have for now, but keep your phone close and charged. And Fortune, your friends are probably already in danger."

"I know."

I disconnected the call and laid the phone on the picnic table, my mind trying to focus on so many things at once. Was Ahmad in New Orleans? Would he show at the Jamison compound? Who was the connection in Sinful? Had we already met?

Then a far-fetched thought flashed through my mind. What if Max was Jamison's man? The money had appeared in Sinful at the same time he had, and someone had killed him and I knew it wasn't Celia. He had a fake ID and he had to have been doing something for money all this time. Something illegal made a lot of sense and explained why he'd never been located.

You're reaching.

I blew out a breath. Was I? Sure, it would be convenient if Max were Jamison's man. No one liked him, he was already dead, and it explained why the money was in Sinful. But it didn't explain why he'd come back to Sinful to begin with. All these years since he'd disappeared, no one had seen Max in Sinful. Why come back now? It couldn't be personal. His business with Celia was over long ago, and wasn't the kind worth revisiting decades later.

I had a feeling that if I could figure out the answer to that question, I could bust this mission wide open. I had a name and address for Max. Hopefully, the address wasn't as fake as the name. That was the first place to start. Just as soon as I could get away from Sinful.

Feeling better now that I had a course of action, I stepped off the picnic table and startled myself when water came right up to the ankles. I shone my flashlight at my feet and saw the bayou swirling around me. The tide must have started coming in while I was talking to Harrison. Something moved to the right of my feet and I directed my penlight that way, praying it wasn't an alligator.

My prayers were answered. It wasn't an alligator.

Unfortunately, it was a snake. A really big snake.

It must have been looking for a place to land because it darted straight for my legs. I tried to jump back onto the picnic table, but it was too late—the snake wrapped around my ankle and clenched as if it had just secured the last raft on the *Titanic*.

I tried not to panic, but all those stories Gertie had told me about water moccasins jumping into hunters' hip waders ran through my mind like the credits to a movie. If that snake headed up my yoga pants, Ahmad wouldn't have to kill me. I'd have a heart attack and die on the spot.

I shook my leg a little, but the snake just tightened more.

Think.

My phone was right where I'd left it on the corner of the picnic table and out of my reach, unless I took a stroll, which didn't seem like the best option given the circumstances. My pistol was in my sports bra, but I couldn't shoot it without shooting myself, so that was out.

I watched as the water moved up another half inch. The snake shifted.

That was it! The snake was trying to get out of the water. If I waded in deeper, he might take off.

Or crawl up higher.

Shit.

There was only one thing left to do. Call for backup.

I wasn't sure yelling would work and I didn't want to take a chance of aggravating the snake, so I did the only smart thing I could do. I shot a round through the bedroom window where Ida Belle was sleeping. I only had a little bit of moonlight to work with, but it was enough to illuminate the outline of the window. I aimed high, and the bullet pierced the glass at one of the top panes. I heard the tinkling of glass and mentally added that to the list of things I had to repair.

I waited to hear commotion from inside the house, but aside from my heavy breathing, it was like a cone of silence had descended on the backyard. Since Merlin had decided to start prowling the house yowling, I knew Ally had put in earplugs before she went to bed, but I had no idea why the other two hadn't responded. I was just about to fire again when I heard the back door creak open.

"Ida Belle?" I half yelled, half cried.

"Fortune?" Ida Belle's voice sounded back. "Where are you?"

"At the picnic table."

"Did you fire that shot?"

Then it clicked. Ida Belle's first assumption was that Ahmad's men had fired the shot. She wasn't ignoring it. She was being cautious. "Yes. That was my cry for help."

Ida Belle turned on her flashlight and started across the yard toward me. "It was a damned loud cry. Almost gave me a heart attack, and you took out one of the globes on the ceiling fan."

"I'll put it on my list, assuming I'm around to make the repairs."

"What the hell is wrong? And what were you doing out here in the first place? Are you stuck?"

"Sorta," I said, figuring answering the last question was the easiest. As Ida Belle stepped up in front of me, I pointed to my foot. "The tide came in and I acquired a passenger."

Ida Belle shone the light on my foot and took a step back. "Holy shit!"

"You are not making me feel better about the situation."

"Sorry. Okay, give me a minute to think."

"In a minute, I'm shooting my own leg off."

"What's all the racket?" Gertie's voice sounded behind us. "I got up to go to the bathroom and heard yelling."

The fact that she'd slept through the gunshot was beyond troubling, but we could address that another time. Assuming I had another time.

"Fortune's got a situation," Ida Belle said.

Gertie tromped across the yard and stepped up beside Ida Belle. "The tide's coming in. Try walking toward the house and you won't be standing in the bayou. This hardly rates yelling, and it was far too simple to be a situation."

"Would you like me to walk in the house with this?" I grabbed her flashlight and trained it on my leg.

Gertie let out a strangled cry and leaped for the picnic table, crawling up to the top to stand. "Holy crap. Shoot it or something."

"I can't without hitting my leg," I said.

"You don't need both of them, do you?" she asked.

"I was kinda thinking I might," I said. "But I'm willing to reconsider."

"Shut up, you two," Ida Belle said. "I'm trying to think."

I stared. "You're telling me you two have never seen this before? It didn't happen to Mary Jo or Billy Bob on the third night of the full moon in March or something and now there's a town law about it?" My voice began to trail up in volume and pitch. I didn't want to admit it, but I was starting to panic a little.

Ida Belle looked up at Gertie. "This isn't a constrictor. Water snakes wrap around things all the time...just usually not a person's legs."

Gertie nodded. "When they jump into hip waders, the person wearing them hops out."

"I can't hop out of my ankle, so we need a different plan."

"The snake is trying to get out of the water," Ida Belle said, "so what about wading in deeper?"

"I thought about that, but what if he runs up my pants leg? All kinds of bad things would happen then."

"Pull up your pants leg first," Gertie said. "If you got it up around your knee there wouldn't be a gap for the snake to get into."

"That's a start," Ida Belle said. "Maybe if you get the pants leg up, then wade in, the snake will loosen a bit, then we can pull it off your leg."

"I do not understand this 'we' of which you speak," Gertie said. "I'm staying right here until all snakes have cleared the area."

"I'll do it, you sissy," Ida Belle said, but she didn't sound completely convinced. "Pull up your pants leg, Fortune."

I sat my pistol on the picnic table and inched the yoga pants up my leg. The snake looked up, but didn't move. So far, so good. I pulled the pants up another couple inches.

"Slow and steady," Gertie said as she leaned over to watch the progress.

"What do you think I'm doing?" I asked and pulled on the pants until they slipped over my knee and stuck.

"Is it tight enough on your leg?" Ida Belle asked.

Slowly, I reached down and rolled the yoga pants over several times, pulling them up on my leg until I darn near cut off the circulation. "It is now. Let's get this over with before my leg goes numb."

"That could be a good thing," Gertie said. "Then you wouldn't feel if the snake bites you."

"Are you ready?" I asked Ida Belle.

She looked at the snake and frowned, then handed Gertie her flashlight. "Give me your nightshirt and make sure you keep that light trained on the snake."

"What?" Gertie said. "I'm not giving you my nightshirt."

"I'm not grabbing that thing bare-handed, and there's no time to go looking for gloves."

"Then use your own nightshirt," Gertie said.

"This is silk," Ida Belle said. "It's not thick enough. Yours is flannel since you're always cold. You sleep in a sports bra. It's no different than being out here in your bathing suit."

"Says the woman who doesn't have to take off her clothes," Gertie grumbled as she pulled her nightshirt over her head and tossed it to Ida Belle.

"Says the woman who has to grab the snake," Ida Belle corrected and wrapped the nightshirt around her right hand and up her forearm. "Okay. I'm ready."

I nodded. "I'm going to step to the right to get out of the way of the picnic table, then I'll step back."

Ida Belle moved in front of me and as I took the step to the side, she mirrored my movement. Gertie stood bent over on the edge of the picnic table, shining the light on my leg.

Ida Belle leaned over, her right hand outstretched and ready to grab. I took a deep breath and blew it out.

"One. Two. Three!"

JANA DELEON

Chapter Nine

I took a big step backward, Ida Belle moving in sync with me. As soon as my leg went underwater, I felt the snake loosen. Ida Belle reached into the water and grabbed the tail of the snake, then pulled. I closed my eyes and waited for the bite that I was sure was coming but instead, the snake unraveled and sprang loose, reaching backward toward Ida Belle. Just before the head made it around to her hand, Ida Belle yelled and flung the snake.

Right at Gertie.

Gertie brandished the flashlight like a sword and attempted to whack the snake away from her, but she lost her balance. She fell off the side of the picnic table, crashing into Ida Belle and me and knocking us all down into the water. All of a sudden, the water thrashed with three sets of frantic, tangled limbs.

"Get off of me!"

"You're on my leg!"

"I can't move!"

"The snake is coming back!"

It was probably only a couple of seconds, but it felt like it took an eternity to get out of the water and run like a madman for dry land. We stopped about twenty feet from the picnic table and stood there, huddled and dripping.

"Who has a flashlight?" I asked.

"I dropped Ida Belle's in the water."

I pulled my penlight out of my pocket and clicked. Nothing.

"It's ruined. Where's your light, Gertie?"

"I think it's still on the picnic table. If I didn't kick it off."

My phone!

I froze as a string of curse words raced through my mind.

"My cell phone was on the picnic table," I said. "I have to have it."

"I'm not going anywhere near that water," Gertie said. "In fact, I'm seriously considering moving to the desert."

"Then there's rattlers," I said.

"At least they give you a warning."

I was just about to head back inside and rustle up another flashlight when a beam of light shone on us from behind. We all turned around, hands over our eyes, trying to see into the light.

"I'm almost afraid to ask," Carter said, "but I suppose it's my job. What the hell is going on here? I got reports of gunfire and screaming, then I show up and the three of you are standing here soaking wet and dressed, well, weird."

I looked over at Gertie, who stood there in her camouflage sports bra and matching underwear, and Ida Belle, who wore some thin, short red silky thing, and then down at my pants leg, which was still wrapped around my thigh.

"I heard a noise and came outside to check it out," I said. "Then a snake wrapped around my leg and I shot my pistol through the bedroom window where Ida Belle was sleeping to get some help."

Carter directed the light down at the ground so that the glow reflected back up but allowed us all to see. He looked at my leg with the offending pants leg. "Is that going numb?"

"A little. Anyway, I left my phone on the picnic table, but we lost our flashlights in the great snake-wrangling adventure, then fell in the water, and now we have no light and I need my phone."

Carter shook his head. "If you had your phone, why didn't you just call for help?"

"Because my phone was out of reach and I was afraid to move, but since my pistol was in my bra, I had a backup plan."

"Your mind is scary on so many levels," Carter said. He directed the flashlight away from us and set off for the picnic table, sloshing in the water as he went. He returned holding my phone, my pistol, and Gertie's small flashlight. "Will you three please go inside and stay there at least until daylight?"

"We can probably manage that," Ida Belle said.

"Please do," Carter said, then looked at me. "Do you realize that every time I get a call about random gunfire in the middle of the night, I automatically start driving this way? I don't even have to hear the address first. What does that tell you?"

"That no one else in Sinful is living it up, apparently," I said.

"I wouldn't call getting my ankle felt up by a snake 'living it up,'" Gertie said, "but it's definitely not boring, like everyone else in this town."

"The entertainment value aside," Carter said, "which was probably high if I'd shown up ten minutes sooner, I'd really appreciate it if you'd become boring until tomorrow."

He turned around and headed across the lawn.

"He's in a mood," Gertie said.

"He hasn't slept in two days," I said. "And everyone who gets a hangnail in this town calls to tell him about it."

"He's exhausted," Ida Belle agreed. "And he's still not fully recovered from the concussion. Then all this business with Celia, the election, the sheriff debacle, and now Max. It's a lot to manage with a full night's sleep and at top-notch health."

"I hadn't thought about all that," Gertie said. "Now I feel a little guilty that he had to come out here, even though for once, it wasn't really my fault." She turned to look at me. "What were you doing out here anyway?"

"Harrison called," I said, seeing no reason to lie about having a call with my partner. I simply wouldn't give them all the details of the call. "I didn't want to risk Ally overhearing, so I came outside. I was sitting on the picnic table and didn't realize the tide was coming in until I stepped off and became a dry dock for the snake."

"What did Harrison say?" Ida Belle asked.

I was about to answer when the back door opened and a flashlight hit us. "What the heck are you guys doing out here?" Ally asked. "Gertie, where are your clothes? Are you all wet? For Christ's sake, get inside before you catch a cold."

"Later," I said.

Ida Belle nodded and we headed for the house.

I was happy for the interruption. It gave me a chance to formulate a reply. The more planned my answer was, the better I was able to let the lies slip off my tongue and have them sound legit. With average people, I could lie on the fly. I'd even managed some doozies with Carter, but then Carter didn't know my true identity. With Ida Belle and Gertie, it was hard to get away with anything. For one, they were trained in the art of deception. For two, they knew who I really was. They would be expecting me to lie to them, and they'd be ready to jump on any twitch or blink that led them to believe I was hiding the truth.

I looked at my cell phone and checked the time. With all the excitement and the lack of air-conditioning, everyone would probably be up at the crack of dawn. That gave me a couple of hours to come up with a way to manage my own involvement in the investigation while keeping them out of it.

I hoped something came to me, because right now, I was drawing a blank.

I spent an hour tossing and turning while trying to come up with a good cover story for Ida Belle and Gertie, and finally dozed off close to dawn. I had just slipped into a solid sleep when the power came back on and everything in the house surged. The air-conditioning roared on, lights flashed, and alarms went on the blink, firing off all over the house.

I jumped out of bed and hit the ground standing, pistol in hand, then relaxed when I realized what had happened. Merlin had leaped straight up when I did and was currently perched on top of the lamp, glaring at me as though it was somehow my fault. A second later, the sound of breaking glass sounded down the hall. I crouched a bit and waited to hear what followed next before heading out. Ally stood frozen across the hall in her bedroom, her eyes wide.

"What the heck are you doing?" Ida Belle yelled. "You're going to kill someone."

"The noise startled me," Gertie said. "It was an accident."

"Why are you sleeping with throwing stars?"

"Turns out it was a better choice than my gun."

"Good God."

I headed out into the hallway, Ally trailing behind me. Ida Belle stood in the doorway of the bedroom Gertie was using, shaking her head in dismay. I peered into the bedroom and saw a hole in one of the windowpanes. Another item for the list. Walter was going to retire off my house repairs.

Gertie climbed out of bed and yanked the cord for the alarm clock out of the wall. "Why was this thing on in the first place?"

"I think there was a power surge," I said. "Things are going off all over the house."

Ida Belle put her fingers in her ears and nodded. "Let's

track them all down and turn them off before we go deaf."

I headed downstairs with Ally, who went to work on the stove, while I went out on the porch and tried to figure out how to shut off the doorbell, which was ringing over and over and over again. I was just contemplating shooting it when Ida Belle walked up behind me with a crowbar and popped the entire thing off the wall.

"Thank God," I said. "I was losing my mind. Is this normal?" I glanced around the neighborhood, but everything was quiet and no one else seemed to be running around in a panic.

Ida Belle shook her head. "I think lightning might have hit the house during the storm. No telling what got fried."

"Crap. You mean fried completely—as in insurance claims and contractors taking over my space?"

"It's possible. We'll start checking everything. The AC seems to be okay. We should probably start in the kitchen."

We headed to the kitchen where Gertie was inspecting the refrigerator. "Seems to be all right," she said as we walked in the room.

Ally closed the door on the microwave. "The stove and oven are good, but the microwave is shot."

"I meant to unplug it," I said. "Guess I forgot."

"At least it's not built in," Ida Belle said. "Easy enough to replace."

"I hope so," I said. "When Ally moves out, the microwave and the coffeepot are the only things that will see activity in this kitchen."

"Coffee!" Gertie pulled the coffeepot away from the wall and heaved a sigh of relief. "You unplugged it. Thank God." She started filling the pot.

Five minutes later, we were all sitting around the kitchen table, silently sipping on coffee and trying to get a focus for the rest of the day.

"You guys never did tell me what happened last night," Ally said. "Why were you in the backyard? What happened to Gertie's clothes? Why were you all wet?"

"I heard a noise and went to investigate," I said, using the same explanation I'd given Carter. Then I told her about the snake and the plan to remove the snake and how it wasn't quite the success we'd hoped for.

Ally started smiling shortly after I started the story, and by the time I got to Gertie falling off the picnic table, she was laughing. By the time I got to Carter spotlighting us all in the backyard, she was gasping for breath. "Oh my God," she said, wiping tears from her eyes. "The things the three of you get into. It's like anything that can go wrong, does, but in such a dramatic way."

"And how fortunate for us that Carter always seems to be around to see it," I said.

"Not always," Gertie said, "which is a good thing. He'd be in a bad mood *all* of the time if he had any idea how many other things we've done."

"I think he has an idea," Ida Belle said. "He just doesn't have proof."

"Well," Ally said, and smiled at me, "your arrival in Sinful has certainly made my life more interesting." She rose from the table. "Since the power's back on, I ought to head down to the café and help Francine. Fingers crossed that all her equipment made it."

"I'm crossing everything," I said. "I need the café open and running at full steam."

I waited until I heard Ally going up the stairs before I spoke again. "Okay, here's the plan. Showers first—that will give Ally time to get dressed and leave. Then Gertie can whip us up some breakfast while I tell you about the call."

Gertie jumped up from the table. "I'm all for that shower part. And an omelet and pancakes sound great after all that red meat."

"If we'd have known the power was coming back on so soon," Ida Belle said, "we would have left that meat in Gertie's freezer. It probably would have been okay."

"Why run the risk?" Gertie said as we headed out of the kitchen. "So we'll eat hamburgers and meat loaf for a while. We've had worse."

"True," Ida Belle agree. "Like the year you decided to try tofu and ordered a truckload thinking it was a trunk load."

I cringed and took the stairs two at a time.

"That was fairly awful," Gertie agreed. "We couldn't even give it away." She stepped onto the landing and sighed. "I guess we don't have to worry about anyone hogging the hot water. This will be speed showering."

Crap. I'd forgotten about the hot water heater being electrical. It had been without power for a day and a half. No way the water would be warm anymore, and it would take hours to heat up again.

I grabbed a towel, stripped, and hopped into the shower. I heard Gertie yelp through the wall to the other bathroom. Despite the fact that the house was still warm, the water was brisk and I found myself wishing my hair was back to the one-inch style I usually sported rather than the long extensions that took a long time to wash and even longer to rinse.

I managed it all in five minutes or so and hopped out of the cold and into a warm fluffy towel. It took another five minutes to dress, get a comb through all the tangles in my hair, and put the entire mess up in a ponytail. Then I headed downstairs for the debriefing, my cover story in place and ready to go.

Gertie was already at the counter, cracking eggs into a bowl. Ida Belle had poured the last of the coffee and was starting another pot. I frowned. It was a sad, sad day when two seniors took less time in the bathroom than I did. I was really losing my edge. I sat down and added sweetener to my coffee, then decided what the hell and poured in some creamer and caramel.

Ida Belle took a seat across from me. "So…Harrison?"

"He and Morrow are working with the FBI in New Orleans. They had some intel on the buyer we suspected was working with Ahmad, a man named Conrad Jamison. The FBI was itching for enough information to take him down. With what we have, they should be able to start building a case."

"That's great," Ida Belle said. "So what's the plan for the takedown?"

"It's not in place yet," I said. "They want to do some recon of the properties owned by the buyer before they decide on a course of action."

"What about Ahmad?"

"MIA, but his men are still in New Orleans."

"And Harrison had no idea why the counterfeit money would be in Sinful?"

I shrugged. "The storm, maybe? It could have been on a boat ready for an exchange or maybe a plane. Either could have crashed given the weather."

Ida Belle frowned and glanced over at Gertie, who shook her head. "I told you," Gertie said.

"Told her what?" I asked.

"That you would try to lie to us," Gertie said, and sighed. "Look, we get it. You don't want us getting hurt, and despite the fact that we'd like to believe that we're still superwomen spies, even I know that I'm way past my prime."

Ida Belle nodded. "But that doesn't mean we can't help.

You don't have to tell us anything about the trap, and we know we can't be anywhere near it when it goes down, but as far as groundwork here goes, there's no reason we can't do what we've always done."

"Meddle," Gertie said.

"I think she's already aware of that," Ida Belle said.

My lips quivered and I finally had to smile. "Yeah, I got the memo."

"You're going to need our help," Ida Belle said. "No one knows more about the people in Sinful than we do. And I know you don't believe that money coincidentally blew into town in a storm."

I blew out a breath. Everything Ida Belle said was true. I knew it would be an uphill battle to figure out the Sinful connection without inside help, and no one was more inside Sinful than Ida Belle and Gertie. But the professional side of me screamed no, and the friend side of me screamed no.

"We're going to get into the middle of it anyway," Gertie said. "You can either call the shots or hope we don't get ourselves into trouble."

"Okay," I said. "I get that you want to help and yes, you've done some really good work before. But this is different. This time I'm performing in my role as a CIA agent, which means I'm directly responsible for you. More importantly, you're my friends and if anything happened to you because of me, I'd never be able to live with myself."

"We understand," Gertie said. "We promise we'll let you call all the shots. We won't do anything that you haven't approved, and we'll report everything we find directly to you."

Ida Belle nodded. "Look, we may just be two senior citizens to everyone else, but you know better. Let us do our job."

I felt a lump form in my throat. It was the same thing I'd

said to Harrison. Gertie and Ida Belle were older and lacked the specialty training I had, but at their core, they were soldiers. At their core, they wanted to make wrongs right. That desire didn't leave just because you got older or slower or your vision got bad.

"I really didn't want to do it without you," I said.

They both smiled.

"Now you're talking," Gertie said. "So what do we do first?"

"I'm strictly assigned to groundwork here in Sinful for now. Director Morrow doesn't want me anywhere near New Orleans. He doesn't want the risk of exposure given that we have no reason to assume that Ahmad knows for certain that I'm in Louisiana."

"Makes sense," Ida Belle said. "Do you have any ideas on where to start?"

"Yeah. It may sound weird, but I'd like to start with Max."

Gertie whirled around, her spatula in the air. "Max?"

Ida Belle's eyes widened. "I have to admit, I didn't see that one coming."

I told them my thoughts about Max's appearance and the strange feeling I had about him having hundreds on him. "I know it doesn't sound like much. Hell, it doesn't sound like anything at all, but I have this feeling."

"Like you did about the money," Ida Belle said.

I nodded.

"Then we check into Max," Ida Belle said. She cocked her head to the side and studied me for several seconds. "You know, it's interesting. With the other things we've gotten involved in, your instincts weren't nearly as sharp, until that arms dealing fiasco. I figured it was because you were in a new place with people that weren't what you normally dealt with. I think I was right."

"Why do you say that?"

"Because as soon as something happened that hit close to home for you, it's like someone flipped a switch. Maybe you've gotten comfortable enough with your environment that your natural state is returning. But it's interesting that something you're connected to is what seemed to jump-start it in a big way. First the arms dealing and now the counterfeit money."

"It's a psychic connection," Gertie said.

Normally, I'd dismiss something like what Gertie said as nonsense, but in this case, I wondered if she was right. I had gotten that tickle in my belly over the arms dealing, and even though the bad guys were all dead or arrested, I couldn't help but feel that the whole story hadn't been told. The money had definitely sent me on high alert. I'd known it was counterfeit long before Harrison verified it. Would have bet real money on it. Now, that same tickle in my belly was telling me that Max had been in this business up to his neck.

"Maybe not necessarily psychic," I said, "but I agree that I have a strong connection to my work. This case has been my entire existence for two years. It makes sense to me that I might feel a 'sameness,' for lack of a better word, about things that are related."

Ida Belle nodded. "Sameness is a good way to describe it. So where do we start with Max?"

"Electricity!" I jumped up from the table and grabbed my laptop off the kitchen counter. "I couldn't look up the address on his fake driver's license last night because we didn't have power and my phone was a loss on Internet searches. Pray that the lightning didn't fry my modem and that the Internet provider is up and running."

I sat back down and opened the laptop. I smiled when I saw full bars for Internet service, then did a maps search for the address on the license. When the address came up, I shifted to satellite mode and zoomed in. Ida Belle moved around next to me and Gertie leaned over my shoulder.

"It's the Warehouse District," Ida Belle said.

"The Warehouse District?" I said. "Why would he live there?"

"People have been rehabbing those old buildings since before Katrina hit," Gertie said. "A lot of areas are businesses on bottom, apartments on top."

"Okay." I opened a new tab and did a search on the address. "It's an art gallery."

"Max always did fancy himself an artist," Ida Belle said.

I slumped back in my chair. "Any chance he actually made it and that's where his money came from all these years?"

"I don't think so," Ida Belle said. "I'm no art critic, but I never saw anything remotely original in his work."

"Wishful thinking, maybe," Gertie said and slid omelets onto the table. "Or perhaps he works there." She took a seat and reached for the salt and pepper. "I'll cook the pancakes after we finish this round."

Ida Belle moved back to her chair and stabbed the omelet with her fork. "I can't imagine Max having the manners or class required to work at an art gallery."

I tapped my fingers on the laptop, then closed it and reached for my plate.

"I know that look," Ida Belle said, "and the answer is no. You cannot go to New Orleans and check out that art gallery. Harrison told you to stay put, remember?"

"He told me to look for the Sinful connection," I said.

"He meant in Sinful," Ida Belle said.

"Yes, but he didn't say I couldn't follow the connection," I argued. "Not specifically." At least, Harrison hadn't said it.

Morrow was a different story.

Ida Belle sighed. "You are as stubborn as they come. If Max is connected to someone buying from Ahmad, then the place may be watched."

"The FBI only has one address, and Harrison didn't say anything about it being an art gallery. He said it was a newspaper or something of the sort. If Jamison owns this gallery, it's buried so well that the FBI hasn't uncovered it yet."

I left out the part where Harrison told me Jamison had crews in charge of his separate business ventures. If Max was wrapped up in this, one of them *could* own the art gallery building or even the art gallery, but his living there was in no way proof that they did.

"For all we know," Gertie said, "Max is renting an upstairs apartment and he picked that location because he liked the idea of pretending he was one of the artists who'd painted work for sale in the shop. It sounds exactly like something he'd do. He always had grandiose ideas."

"But married Celia," I said.

"Celia had that inheritance, though, and Max liked what money could buy him," Ida Belle said. "He probably never imagined being married to her would be so difficult. Men tend to underestimate women in most areas."

"True."

Ida Belle lowered her fork. "Gertie is right, though. Living above an art gallery is just the sort of thing Max would have done."

Gertie nodded. "He's probably got some of those awful landscapes he used to paint upstairs, pretending he's the next big undiscovered thing."

The suggestion made total sense. From everything I'd seen of Max, he'd certainly seemed full of himself, and if he fancied himself an artist, then living above an art gallery was another way to feed his self-delusion. Besides, we hadn't even established that Max was the Sinful connection, so the entire discussion could be a moot point.

"So if I had a disguise," I said, "there's no reason I shouldn't be able to get in and out without anyone being the wiser."

"The only disguises you've worn while you were here were the kind that made you blend at the Swamp Bar," Ida Belle said. "That same outfit will get you arrested for prostitution in the Warehouse District."

"I was thinking something more nondescript," I said. "Like a UPS uniform."

"Oh!" Gertie's eyes widened. "That's a really good idea. People don't even look at deliverymen...or women."

"And how do you plan on getting a UPS uniform?" Ida Belle asked. "I don't think they hand them out just because someone asks."

"It's a tan shirt and trousers or shorts. Surely one of you has something we could make work. I can draw their logo on white material and Gertie can sew it on. It doesn't have to pass inspection at UPS. It just has to be close enough that people don't look twice."

"Ida Belle had a safari outfit last Halloween," Gertie said. "That would work."

Ida Belle frowned. "I don't know...it just seems like a big risk."

"Trust me," I said. "If I can sorta pull off librarian-ex-beauty-queen, UPS delivery girl is a cakewalk."

Finally Ida Belle nodded. "I suppose it's worth a shot, but that's assuming you'll be able to get in at all. With Max's death being a murder, Carter might have asked the New Orleans police to seal off the apartment."

"Let's hope he hasn't gotten that far, or didn't deem it necessary," I said.

"Hmmm." Ida Belle narrowed her eyes at me. "If we get there, and police tape is across that door, we're turning around and coming back home."

"Of course," I said as soon as I made sure my ankles were crossed.

"I mean it," Ida Belle said. "No risk taking. Not on this one."

I nodded and looked across the table at Gertie, who winked.

Game on.

Chapter Ten

Three hours later, we were crammed in Gertie's car and headed for New Orleans. Ida Belle's safari outfit had worked perfectly. I'd nailed the freehand of the logo. Unless someone got too close for comfort, no one was going to look twice at me. I even had a small box with a UPS label on it from Gertie. That woman kept everything. Tennis shoes and sunglasses completed the look.

I'd told Carter we were making a trip to New Orleans for supplies rather than waiting to order them and asked if we could pick him up anything. He suggested a new toilet would be nice, and since Gertie had been the source of the restroom problems down at the sheriff's department, I told him we'd see what we could do.

We stopped at the hardware store on the way. No one wanted to admit that we were getting the supplies first because things might go wrong and we'd have to make a getaway, but we all knew that was the reason.

I had to order the glass for my windows, but that didn't surprise me. The house was old and the windows were the originals with individual panes. It was pretty but sorta a hassle. If I actually cleaned, I'd probably hate them. As it was, the entire place was in need of a good spring cleaning. I might check into hiring someone as soon as things settled down. Technically, it wasn't my house as I wasn't really Marge's niece, but since I was benefiting from staying there, it only seemed right that I keep the place from falling apart, especially as I'd been the root cause of the recent damage.

We finished up our shopping and carted everything back to Gertie's car. "I still can't believe you made me buy this," Gertie said as she closed the trunk over the new white toilet inside.

"It's the least you owe the man," Ida Belle said. "You ought to be buying him new clothes and paying for therapy. In less than a ten-hour span, he tackled a toilet and got sprayed with toilet water, then saw you in your skivvies. When you deliver that, it should be with a big bottle of whiskey."

Gertie waved a hand in dismissal and I grinned as I climbed into the backseat next to bags from the hardware store.

"So everyone knows what they're doing, right?" I said.

"I'm sitting in the car," Gertie said, "waiting for you and Ida Belle to come out, then I drive back home. It's not like you've set me out to solve the Da Vinci Code or something."

Gertie was still a little perturbed that she hadn't been tasked with something more important than driving the car, but I'd finally convinced her that getaway driver was an important role. The unfortunate part was, Gertie was scary as hell as the getaway driver, but I was less afraid of her behind the wheel than inside the art gallery.

Ida Belle had borrowed a wig from a friend of hers and pulled it on, checking herself in the mirror. "I'll enter the art gallery and pretend to shop. I'll ask about the artists and see if I can determine who owns the gallery and the building. How do I look?" She turned around to look at me.

"It's amazing what a difference hair style and color makes," I said. The wig Ida Belle had borrowed was a chin-length bob in a dark glossy brown. It took a good fifteen years off her. "It makes you look younger."

"Let me see," Gertie said and looked over at Ida Belle. "You still look old and grouchy to me."

"You're just jealous," Ida Belle said and looked at herself in the mirror. "I suppose I do look a bit younger."

"Ten years younger than the Walking Dead, maybe," Gertie groused.

I sighed. Thank God we were only a couple minutes from the art gallery. Gertie's complaining was getting old. When we got back to Sinful, we were going to have to find something special for her to do, or Ida Belle and I would be listening to her go on like this for days.

Gertie let me out of the car around the corner and then proceeded past the art gallery and parked at the curb a couple buildings down. I headed up the street with my package as Ida Belle exited the car and entered the gallery. Our hope was that the gallery only had one employee working and that Ida Belle's distracting them with questions would be enough to keep them from focusing on me.

The gallery was a long, fairly narrow room with paintings hanging on both sides of the walls. Long panels divided the room in two and contained more artwork on each side. Ida Belle was the only patron inside, and she was standing in front of a large painting of the swamp and talking to a young man sporting ear gauges and a bunch of facial piercings.

Five feet eight. A hundred forty pounds, including the jewelry. No threat unless he stabbed me with a piercing.

The gallery employee glanced over at the door as I entered and I was happy to note the door didn't make a sound. No signal for entry or departure worked in my favor.

"Package for Thomas Johnson," I said, taking on my bored and slightly impatient expression.

"Upstairs," the young man said and pointed to a staircase at the rear of the building. "It's the unit on the right, but I haven't seen him for a couple days. He might not be at home."

"I don't need a signature," I said. "I'll leave it at the door."

The young man shrugged, clearly unconcerned with Thomas Johnson or his packages. When he turned back around, I inclined my head to the other side of the room and Ida Belle nodded. Then I headed for the staircase. So far, so good. With Ida Belle moving Piercing Boy to the back side of the panels, he would assume he missed my leaving, if he thought about it at all.

I bounded up the stairs and located the apartment and smiled. No police tape. Either Carter hadn't had a chance to contact the New Orleans police about Max's death or more likely, the locals were busy with issues from the storm and hadn't had a chance to check. After all, Max was already dead, and he hadn't been murdered in their jurisdiction. With no reason to suspect Max was involved in bigger crimes, his murder wouldn't be a priority.

A quick inspection of the lock made me even happier. Whoever had renovated the building had followed the general rule of contracting and used cheap locks for the doors. I would have this open in no time. I pulled on my gloves, then went to work. Using nothing but a credit card and a stiff wire, it took only a couple of seconds to get the lock open. I peered inside to make sure it was clear, then stepped into the apartment, closing and locking the door behind me.

The apartment was a studio type, which was another thing on the plus list. Small meant easier to search, and Max had apparently gone for the minimalist look, at least as far as furniture went. The walls were a completely different story. They were littered with paintings—big, medium, small, oils, acrylics, chalk, pencil, landscapes, portraits, fruit in bowls. I felt like I was being suffocated by an art school.

I tossed the package onto an incredibly uncomfortable-looking white modern couch and pulled open a drawer on the end table. Nothing but a television remote inside. I moved into the kitchen and checked the drawers and cabinets, but all I discovered is that Max didn't cook or clean. He had zero cooking utensils and his refrigerator was disgusting. Things had been growing in there for quite some time.

I moved into the makeshift bedroom, which consisted of a mattress and one nightstand in the far corner of the apartment. The top drawer of the nightstand held a couple of skin magazines and a couple pairs of socks. The bottom drawer held underwear. I shifted them around, glad I was wearing gloves, but didn't see anything else. I tapped the bottom of the drawers, as I'd done all the others, but there were no false bottoms and nothing was taped underneath.

I moved on to the bathroom, but it held only a toilet, shower, and pedestal sink, so no hiding places available other than a medicine cabinet that contained only basic toiletries and the toilet tank, which was clear. At the back of the bathroom was a skinny door that I figured must be the closet. I pulled it open and saw some jeans and T-shirts and a couple of cheap suits and shoes. I pushed everything around, digging in pockets and inside the shoes, then pressed the walls to make sure no hiding places existed, then closed the closet and headed back into the living room.

I stood in the middle of the room and looked around, feeling completely unsatisfied. This was all wrong. Nothing about this place besides the artwork indicated that Max lived here. Otherwise, the place could have belonged to any single male with questionable hygiene and bad taste in clothes. It was so sterile, it had to be intentional. Not a single checkbook or piece of mail. Not an insurance card, a set of car keys, or a single photo.

If it hadn't been for the thick layer of dust covering everything, I would have assumed he'd recently moved in and hadn't finished unpacking. Max may have rented this place, and he probably slept and showered here, but it wasn't where he conducted business. Everyone had personal papers, even criminals. He must have all of it stored somewhere else.

My cell phone buzzed and I pulled it out, hoping nothing had gone awry. It was Gertie.

You find anything?

I texted back.

No. The entire place is completely devoid of indication of who occupies it. Not a single personal document.

A couple seconds later, Gertie replied.

He used to hide things behind paintings. Are there any hanging in there?

I glanced around the apartment and groaned.

Are you kidding me? It looks like the Louvre threw up its rejects in here.

I slipped the cell phone back into my pocket and started systematically removing the paintings one at a time and checking the back. At this rate, I'd be here all afternoon. When I finished the first wall, I moved on to the next. I pulled a particularly large and incredibly tacky painting of dogs playing poker off the wall from behind the couch and carefully stepped off the couch with it, making sure I didn't drop it or take out a lamp. I leaned it against the wall and immediately spotted the pouch on the back.

It was one of those golden mailing envelopes and it was attached to the back of the frame by a Velcro strap. I removed the envelope and checked the contents.

Finally!

The envelope was full of hundred-dollar bills.

I mentally cursed myself for not bringing a magnifying glass, but I wasn't sure it mattered. As soon as I saw the money, I got that feeling again—my Spidey sense—telling me it was no coincidence.

I took a couple bills out of the envelope and put the rest back. I placed my hands under the crossbar that ran across the middle of the painting and was just about to heft it back on the wall when my fingers brushed against something solid on the back side of the crossbar. I shifted my fingers to the side and felt what appeared to be a solid block of wood attached to the back of the crossbar.

Some sort of bracing, maybe?

Except that after about eight inches, the block ended, which meant it couldn't be supporting anything. I bent over for a better look and saw a dark block of something that looked like metal attached to the back of the crossbar. I ran my fingers down it again and this time felt a ribbon that ran around it. I traced the ribbon to where it was tied at the bottom of the crossbar and picked it apart with my fingers.

My excitement grew as I worked on the ribbon. Whatever this was, it was important enough that Max had gone to a lot of trouble to hide it. A small box of documents, maybe? Fake IDs, a list of contacts, addresses of businesses?

Finally, I got the ribbon loose and the block slipped from behind the crossbar and into my hand. I pulled it out and stared in surprise.

It was a counterfeit die.

I pulled it in for a closer look and could see it was for a collectible coin, but I couldn't identify which one.

Part of the mystery fell into place. Max's disappearance with no visible means of support. His focus on reproductive art rather than creative. The fake bills in his wallet and his apartment. Their appearance in Sinful at the same time he returned.

Max wasn't part of the arms dealing crew. He was the counterfeiter.

He'd probably started with the coins. They were easier to trade in small amounts and as long as you didn't take them to a serious collector. He'd probably managed a good living off of that alone. But counterfeiting bills took a serious investment of equipment, if you wanted to do it right. And the hundreds were some of the best I'd ever seen. Printing money for arms dealers was a lucrative business, especially if you were the artist, but it was also a dangerous one. Once the artwork was complete, the artist wasn't a necessary expense any longer, but he usually wasn't killed, either. Something must have happened to put Max on a hit list.

Like Ahmad's discovering the money was fake due to the mistakes.

Max's not-quite-good-enough artistic ability may be what had bought him two shotgun shells in the chest. But that still didn't answer the question of what Max was doing in Sinful.

My phone buzzed and I pulled it out to check. It was Gertie again.

Police just pulled up and are on their way inside gallery.

Holy crap!

The inside stairs were the only way out I'd seen, and no way could I get by the police without them seeing me. And if they saw me, they'd stop me for questioning, especially if the art gallery employee told them I was delivering a package to a dead man and should have been gone twenty minutes ago.

I started to lift the painting back on the wall, but stopped. No way I could get it back up and straight before the police broke the door down, and what did it matter anyway? Not like Max was going to sue me for ransacking his property. I placed the dies on the end table and hauled butt for the window at the back of the apartment, praying there was something to use to get out. I was capable of dropping two stories, but it wasn't preferred.

I lifted the window and looked out. A drainpipe was a foot away from the window, running down the side of the building into the alley. I started to climb out the window when I remembered the fake UPS package. Crap! My fingerprints were all over it.

I ran back to the couch and grabbed the package. I could hear footsteps coming up the stairs. The cops would be here any minute. I ran to the window and tossed the package out, then reached for the drainpipe, and that's when I saw two men in suits, standing in the alley and looking up at me.

Six feet two and six feet three. Two hundred forty and two hundred sixty pounds. Very little body fat. Armed and deadly as hell.

They weren't law enforcement. Something about the stance was different. But they were definitely interested in Max's apartment. Which meant they were probably either Jamison's men or Ahmad's. Neither worked out well for me.

I pulled out my phone and texted Gertie.

Police about to open door. Bad guys in alley. Can't leave through window.

I have no idea what I thought Gertie could do about the situation, but I prayed she came through with one of her plans that didn't quite work the way she intended but got us all out alive. One of the guys in the alley pointed at me and I could hear them arguing, but I couldn't make out what they were saying and couldn't see their lips clearly from my perch on the window.

I was just weighing my options of facing the police and having to return to DC via the New Orleans police or facing the bad guys outside and hoping they didn't shoot me when I heard tires squealing. I looked down the alley and saw Gertie's Cadillac barreling toward the two men, knocking trash cans everywhere as she went.

As she got near the building, she veered toward me, forcing the two men to jump to the other side of the alley to avoid being hit. I swung my legs over the window ledge and said a quick prayer as I jumped.

Chapter Eleven

My timing was excellent, because I landed square in the middle on top of the Cadillac. Gertie accelerated again and I heard the men yelling behind me as the first bullet whizzed by my head. I rolled to the side of the car, tucked into the window and dropped into the passenger's seat. Gertie yanked the wheel to the right and we tore out of the alley. We were halfway down the next street when I heard a car roar to life and looked back to see a black sedan squeal away from the curb.

"They're following us!" I shouted.

Gertie glanced in the rearview mirror. "Glove box!"

I opened the glove box and found a small arsenal. A nine-millimeter, a .45, a flare gun, and God forbid, a grenade.

I wasn't about to risk hitting a civilian with the nine, so I grabbed the flare gun and fired it at their hood. The flare screamed out of the gun and landed right in the middle of their windshield.

"Bull's-eye!" Gertie yelled.

I was just about to fire again when I heard a crash. A second later, the porcelain toilet appeared behind Gertie's car, rolling down the street. The men's vision had been compromised by the flare and they didn't see the toilet until it was too late. They hit it head-on, and the sedan slid sideways and crashed into a Dumpster. Gertie made a hard right onto the next street, then a left on the next as I watched over the seat.

"I think we lost them," I said and turned around to flop down in the passenger's seat.

"We lost them and the darn toilet." Gertie shook her head in dismay.

"I thought you had your trunk bottom fixed." When I'd first arrived in Sinful, there had been an unfortunate incident during which I'd been required to ride in the trunk. Even more unfortunate had been when the bottom fell out of it, dropping me to the ground right in front of Carter, who was the person I was trying to hide from.

"I sorta fixed it," Gertie said.

I nodded. Gertie was sorta known for sorta fixing things. "Well, this is one of those rare times when your lack of attention to proper maintenance paid off."

"Except for the part where we don't have a toilet for Carter."

"I'll tell him the trunk bottom is missing, and it wouldn't fit in the backseat. That's all true enough. At least, it is now." I sat up straight in my seat. "Crap! We left Ida Belle!"

I was just pulling my phone out of my pocket when Gertie's phone signaled she'd received a text. I grabbed her phone from the center console and checked it.

Did you two get away?

"It's Ida Belle," I said and sent a text back.

Barely. Where are you?

I'm taking Uber. Pick me up at the French Market.

I heaved a sigh of relief. "We need to pick her up at the French Market."

"Good. Since I've been weaving up and down streets like a drunk, we're only a couple blocks away."

She turned down Governor Nicholls Street and pulled up to the corner and stopped. Ida Belle waved from across the street, then ran across and hopped in the backseat.

"You have no idea how happy I am to see the two of you in one piece and not in the back of a police car," Ida Belle said as Gertie pulled away from the curb. "When the cops came into the gallery, I almost had a heart attack, but I couldn't think of any way to distract them. Then all the commotion started and then gunfire. The cops came running back downstairs and that idiot with the piercings locked himself in the bathroom, wailing like a baby. I hauled butt to look out the back door just in time to see you slide off the roof of Gertie's car. I figured it was a darn good time to get the hell out of there, so I left through the front door, jogged a block away, and called Uber. What happened?"

"There were two men in the alley," Gertie said. "They were watching Max's place, so Fortune couldn't get out the back window. I pulled a drive-by and she did a circus leap onto the top of the car."

Ida Belle shook her head, staring at me in admiration. "I figured as much, but hearing it's true just makes it that much more impressive. Did you recognize the men?"

"No," I said, "and I got a good look at them."

"How did you get away?" Ida Belle asked.

"Carter's toilet took them out," Gertie said and started giggling.

Ida Belle stared at her as if she'd lost her mind, so I explained the situation with the sorta-repaired trunk and the now-destroyed toilet.

"You are a menace to society," Ida Belle said, smiling.

"And it's a darn good thing," Gertie said. "No way I could have outrun those guys. If that toilet hadn't taken them out, then Fortune would have had to use the grenade."

"You have a grenade?" Ida Belle looked a tiny bit scared.

"Of course," Gertie said. "I keep one in my glove box."

"Okay," Ida Belle said. "We'll shelve that one for discussion later on." She looked at me. "Did you find anything?"

"Oh yeah." I told them about the money and the dies.

Their eyes widened. "You think Max was the counterfeiter?" Ida Belle asked.

I nodded. "It would explain a lot of things—why he had the counterfeit bills on him when he was killed, what he's done to support himself all these years—"

"Why someone wanted to kill him," Gertie said.

"Yeah, that too," I agreed.

"So the guys could have been from either camp," Ida Belle said. "Were they Middle Eastern?"

"I didn't recognize them, but they both had dark hair and tanned skin," I said. "They could be Middle Eastern, Creole, Italian, or regular white boys with dark hair and a really good tan. I couldn't hear their voices well enough to tell if they had an accent. It was all muddled."

"You didn't get a feel for one or the other?" Ida Belle asked.

"The only feeling I had was an 'oh shit' one," I said.

"Well," Ida Belle said, "I guess that answers some questions about Max."

"But leaves the biggest one unanswered," I said. "We still don't know why he came back to Sinful."

"Maybe he left something in Celia's house," Gertie said. "Maybe he was working on counterfeiting stuff way back then and left something behind."

"Even so," I said, "why come back for it now? He's had a long time to retrieve anything he might have left here. And even if that was the case, why stroll into town announcing his presence? If he was there to lift something, why get everyone looking at him? He could have sneaked back when Celia was off on vacation and accomplished retrieving something he left with no witnesses and no drama."

"And no death," Ida Belle said. "I still think he came back to see someone."

"But who?" Gertie asked. "And is that person the one who shot him or did someone follow him to Sinful?"

"On that same train of thought," I threw in, "if someone followed him to Sinful and killed him, who are they working for?"

Ida Belle blew out a breath. "There's too many missing pieces."

I nodded. "We have to figure out who Max saw while he was in Sinful. He couldn't have been anywhere public without people watching. If we knew everyone he talked to, then maybe we could figure out more of the story."

"I'll put word out to the Sinful Ladies as soon as we get back and see what they know."

"Good," I said. "Did you find out anything from Piercing Boy?"

Ida Belle rolled her eyes. "What a piece of work he was. Complained the entire time about how he worked like a slave for the gallery but they wouldn't feature his own work. I was just about to tell him to stuff it when I figured I could use it to my advantage. I told him that was outrageous and if he'd give me the name of the gallery owner, I'd be happy to call and let them know that I'd seen Piercing's work and thought it would be a great addition to the gallery."

"Did he buy it?"

"Of course. Egotistical people are unable to comprehend anyone who doesn't see their greatness. He said the gallery was owned by an investment group but a man named Owen Randal was in charge of it."

"Do either of you know the name?" I asked.

They both shook their heads.

"Well, it's a place to start," I said. "We can look deeper into this Randal and into Max's fake identity. Maybe we'll come up with more connections."

"Let's hope it's the Sinful connection," Ida Belle said. "If Max was involved with someone in Sinful, I want that person exposed as soon as possible."

I frowned. Not because I disagreed with Ida Belle. I was in total agreement on that one. If Max had a business contact in Sinful, I wanted them outed as quickly as possible. What worried me now was something completely different.

"What's wrong?" Ida Belle said. "You have that look again."

"I'm just wondering if the guys in the alley got a good enough look at Gertie's license plate to trace it."

Gertie sucked in a breath and Ida Belle shot a worried look in her direction.

"They were close enough to see it," Gertie said.

"But were they paying attention?" Ida Belle said. "With everything else that was going on, maybe not."

"But maybe they were," I said. "I think we need to proceed with the assumption that they got the license plate. That's the only safe way to play this."

Ida Belle nodded. "Gertie needs to park the car in her driveway and stay with me."

"When they realize she's not staying at her house," I said, "the first place they'll look is your place. All they'd have to do is ask anyone in town where they might find her and the answer will be with you."

"Well, we can't stay with you," Ida Belle said, "or we'll lead them straight to you and Ally. Besides which, what possible excuse could we have for both bunking at your place? Power is back on. Our houses weren't damaged. What would you tell Ally or Carter, for that matter? He's bound to wonder why you suddenly look like a bed-and-breakfast."

"I suppose a bunch of grown women don't have slumber parties," I said.

"Oh!" Gertie perked up. "I love slumber parties."

"*Most* grown women don't have slumber parties," Ida Belle said.

She was right, of course. It would look odd and at the moment, I didn't have a single good explanation for becoming a hotel.

"How about this," I said. "In the daytime, it doesn't matter where we are as long as we're in sight of other people and stick together, right?"

"Yes," Ida Belle agreed.

"So during the day, we help clean up debris, which gives us a chance to gossip with different people about Max. At night, we go to my house because I've still got enough ground meat to feed an army, then we get drunk and everyone stays over."

"I especially like the part where we all get drunk," Gertie said.

"After that car chase," I said, "a shot of whiskey sounds good about now."

"A shot of whiskey always sounds good when you live in Sinful," Ida Belle said. She pointed her finger at Gertie. "You need to set your house alarm. No excuses this time."

I stared at Gertie. "You have a house alarm?"

Gertie waved a hand in dismissal. "One of those scaredy-cat women at church insisted. Her husband was an installer and all I paid for was the equipment."

"Where's the keypad?" I asked as I mentally scanned the walls of Gertie's house.

"It's in the coat closet," Gertie said.

"Why?" I asked.

"That crazy woman insisted that if it was on an open wall someone could look through the window and see me put in my code."

"She sounds a little paranoid," I said.

"She's a lot paranoid," Gertie said. "Unfortunately, she owed me a favor and that was the only way I could get her to leave me alone."

"You're still paying for the monitoring service, right?"

"Yeah," Gertie said.

Ida Belle sighed. "Something you never use. I realize that most of the time it's not necessary, but this is one of those times when I think you should turn it on. If nothing else, it will scare them away."

I nodded. "I agree. And if it scares them away before they get inside, then it still leaves them thinking you're in the house."

"Which means they won't go looking for you somewhere else," Ida Belle said.

"Fine," Gertie said. "I'll turn the darn thing on, but I take no responsibility if it goes off at stupid hours. I never could get it to work right before, which is why I stopped using it at all."

"If it goes off in the middle of the night," I said, "you can always blame it on storm damage. That should help your neighbors get over any interruption."

"Okay," Ida Belle said. "This whole drunken slumber party plan might work for a day or two, but after that, we'll have to figure out something else."

"Let's cross that bridge when we come to it," I said.

What I really hoped was that in a couple of days, this entire thing would be over and we'd never come to that bridge at all.

###

Ally was still at the café when we got back to Sinful, so we broke out my laptop and started researching Thomas Johnson and Owen Randal. It took only a couple of minutes to give up on Max's fake identity. The first and last name were both common. Put them together and the number of hits was astronomical. It would have taken a thousand people a thousand years to comb them all, and there was still no guarantee anything would pertain to Max.

Owen Randal yielded more results.

"Mr. Randal is a very busy man," I said as we ran through the list of businesses we found him associated with. "Two art galleries, three restaurants, two bars, and a funeral home."

"The funeral home thing is creepy," Gertie said.

"Someone has to own them," Ida Belle said.

"Yeah, but it's creepy when it's someone who might also be creating customers," Gertie said.

"Definitely an unfair advantage," I agreed, "but also a good way to transport illegal goods. No one wants to open a coffin and look inside without a really good reason."

Ida Belle nodded. "And stuff is smuggled in paintings all the time. They don't x-ray everything at customs."

"The restaurants and bars are good for laundering small amounts of cash at a time," I said. "But all of this is speculation. For all we know, this Randal could be an upstanding citizen with eclectic investment taste."

Ida Belle tapped my screen. "Except for the part where he's a criminal."

I looked at the bottom of the screen at the link she was pointing to.

Local Businessman Arrested

That sounded promising. I clicked on the link.

Local businessman Owen Randal was arrested a week ago and

questioned on racketeering charges. Insiders say Randal was held overnight and released the next morning. Despite rumors of Randal's illegal activities, the DA appears unwilling to bring charges against the man who, because of his flamboyant personality, has been referred to by some as the Louisiana John Gotti.

"Racketeering," Ida Belle said and looked at me. "Are you thinking what I'm thinking?"

"That Randal might be one of Jamison's point men, specifically the one who handles the counterfeit money and laundering portion of the business."

"If Randal is the real deal, then the Heberts will have the scoop on him," Gertie said.

"I don't know," I said. "I worry though about forming too much of a dependence on the Heberts for information. Despite the fact that they've helped us a lot, they're still not the good guys."

"True," Ida Belle said, "but this is a simple question. We're not asking for background checks or airboats."

"I know, but it still makes me nervous," I said. "The Heberts have seen me in action enough times to question my background story. If they get too curious, they could blow my cover without even meaning to."

Ida Belle frowned. "You're probably right. If you're constantly poking your nose into every crime connected with Sinful, then they might start to wonder why. When it's personal, you have an excuse, but Max wasn't anyone to you. He wasn't much of anyone to anyone, to be quite honest."

"So we put the Heberts as plan B," I said, "but the first thing we need to do is see if we can connect Randal to anyone in Sinful."

"I can help with that," Gertie said and pulled my laptop over in front of her.

"You can help?" Ida Belle said. "Just like that?"

Gertie nodded and started typing. "If the connection is related to Randal, then yes. If it's strictly a business thing, then no."

I leaned over to check the screen. "Ancestry.com?"

"I started researching my family tree," Gertie said, looking excited. "I'm convinced I'm related to ancient warriors. I just have to track them down."

I looked over at Ida Belle, who shook her head. Apparently, it was a conversation that didn't need to happen. At least not right now. "So," I said, "this will tell you who Randal is related to?"

"If people have linked him to family tree work. It's like one big giant blackboard of families that anyone with a membership can access."

"So people all over the world can contribute to one tree?" I asked. "That's a great concept." I wondered briefly if anyone had ever connected my mom and dad to a branch of their family tree. My parents had always contended we had no living family, but that couldn't possibly be true, right? Everyone had a fourth cousin or crazy great-aunt somewhere. Maybe when all this was over, I'd have Gertie show me how to use the site and see if I had any living relatives. If any of them were like my mom, it might be nice to know them.

"Here we go," Gertie said and pointed to the screen. "Someone linked an Owen Randal, born 1975, to the Piedmont family."

"Are there any Piedmonts in Sinful?" I asked.

"Not that I know of," Ida Belle said.

"Wait!" Gertie pointed to the screen and clapped. "Gracie Piedmont married Brody Sampson in 1985."

"I take it you know the Sampsons?" I asked.

"Gracie and Brody live a couple blocks from here," Ida Belle said.

"That's not the best part," Gertie said. "Brody and Max were best buddies."

"Until he married Celia," Ida Belle said. "Gracie hated Celia with a passion and forbade Brody to hang out with him when she married Max."

"He didn't listen, though," Gertie said. "We used to see them fishing together near Number Two."

"Is this Brody a shady sort?" I asked.

"Not that I know of," Ida Belle said. "He's the local postman. She teaches piano lessons. I've never heard of either of them being involved in anything questionable, but then that seems to be the theme around here lately."

"Maybe it's nothing," I said, "but we should check them out. Are you guys on the outs with either of them?"

"Gracie is a member of the Baptist church," Gertie said. "She helps out with charity events and such. She's always been pleasant to me."

Ida Belle nodded. "I'm not sure she's capable of anything else. She's one of those woman that you can only take a small dose of—too nice, if you know what I mean."

Gertie rolled her eyes. "Only you would consider 'nice' a character flaw."

"*Too* nice," Ida Belle said. "There's a difference."

"Well, then I suggest we start on that block checking on people to help out," I said. "Maybe this Gracie isn't as nice as Ida Belle thinks she is."

"Or maybe Brody took advantage of her connection to Randal," Gertie said, "and is looking for a better retirement than the post office provides."

"Only one way to find out," I said and hopped up from the

dining table. "First, we'll get whatever you guys need from your houses, and drop off Gertie's car. I don't want you guys going back to your homes until we know the coast is clear."

I hoped it was soon.

Chapter Twelve

Gracie and Brody were removing bushes from their front yard when we parked my Jeep at the curb. Gracie looked up and waved at us, wearing a big smile. Brody looked less enthusiastic. Or depending on your view, he looked appropriately enthusiastic given the job he was currently performing in the heat and humidity of July after a tropical storm.

I sized him up first.

Fiftyish. Six feet tall. Two hundred twenty pounds. Decent forearm strength. Weak legs.

I gave her a glance, which was all I needed.

Fiftyish. Smiles way too big. Harmless.

"We're making the rounds," Ida Belle said as we walked up. "Seeing who needs help clearing debris."

"That's so nice of you," Gracie said. "Isn't it, Brody?"

Brody grunted, barely looking up from his stack of tree limbs.

Gracie locked her gaze on me and stepped forward, a gloved hand outstretched. "I don't think we've met. I'm Gracie Sampson. You must be Fortune. I've heard so much about you."

I shook her hand. "Only good stuff, I hope."

Gracie smiled. "I don't listen to anything bad. Negativity hurts my ears."

"Then you must be in pain a lot," I said.

She laughed. "I heard you had a great sense of humor. All

that beauty and a personality, too. The local girls better hide their husbands."

I glanced over at Ida Belle, who rolled her eyes.

Too nice.

I totally wanted to shoot her.

"I think the husbands are safe," I said. "Anyone who'd cheat on his wife is not someone I'm interested in spending time with."

Gracie nodded. "Isn't that the truth?"

"Well," Gertie said, "there's that and then there's the part where she's dating Carter."

"Ohhhhhh." Gracie's mouth formed an O. "He's so handsome and so mannered. His mother did a great job raising him."

I nodded.

"So Brody," Ida Belle said, shifting the conversation, "you must have been surprised when your old high school buddy turned up."

"Even more surprised when he turned up dead," Gertie said.

Ida Belle elbowed her in the ribs as Brody ran one gloved hand over the top of his head.

"Yeah," he said. "I was pretty surprised all the way around. Still not sure what to think of it."

Gracie, who'd been frowning ever since Ida Belle had dropped the Max bomb, shook her head. "I know exactly what to think of it. Max married that horrible woman and she made his life miserable. I don't know why he wanted to come back here after he got away."

"Maybe because it's still where he considers home?" I suggested.

Gracie sniffed. "I'm sure there's some truth to that. I

suppose if I moved away from Sinful, no place else would ever feel the same to me, even if I lived the rest of my life there. But look what it cost him. Nothing is worth dying over, especially Celia Arceneaux."

"You don't think he came back because of Celia, do you?" Ida Belle asked. "Lord, I figured that ship had sailed years ago, and after how mean he was to her at the café…it sure didn't sound like a man trying to make amends for a bad decision."

"Heavens!" Gracie said. "I don't think he was here to win back Celia's heart. I'm not even convinced she has one."

"Me either," Gertie grumbled.

"Then I don't follow," Ida Belle said.

Gracie sighed. "He was killed in Celia's house. There wasn't any power and they're about the same size. Obviously, someone thought he was Celia."

I considered this for a moment. As far as theories went, it was a fairly interesting one and not easy to completely dismiss. I didn't think it was correct, but it was an angle I hadn't previously considered.

"But who would want to kill Celia?" I asked.

Gertie snorted. "Who wouldn't?"

Gracie nodded and I held in a smile. For someone who claimed to avoid negativity, Gracie was a big fail when it came to Celia.

"I don't know," I said. "I mean, there's probably plenty of people who wouldn't shed a tear if Celia was gone, but there's a big gap between hating someone, or even wishing them dead, and actually killing them."

It was a mantra I'd spoken more than once and thought about all the time, especially given my profession. But civilians always seemed a bit taken aback at it. Gracie was no exception.

Her eyes widened and she stared at me for several

uncomfortable seconds. "I guess I hadn't considered it all the way through," Gracie said.

"Of course you didn't," Gertie said. "You can't fathom actually killing someone, which is a good thing."

"That's true," Gracie said, "but I still think Celia had more enemies in this town than Max. He's been gone for over twenty years. Why would someone wait all this time to settle an old score with him?"

"Maybe it's the first opportunity they got," Ida Belle said. "He *did* disappear." She looked over at Brody, who'd been quiet during our entire exchange. "Did you get a chance to talk to Max when he returned?"

Brody didn't answer for a couple of seconds, and I started to wonder if he'd even heard the question. Finally, he came out of his stupor and nodded. "Briefly."

Gracie frowned. "You didn't tell me that."

"Because it wasn't worth telling," Brody said. "He was coming out of the café and saw me across the street. He came over to say hi but before we could get past the small talk of how many years it had been and the storm that was coming, he got a phone call and excused himself. He said he'd swing by later to catch up, but I guess he didn't have time to make it by before the storm."

And now he wouldn't be making it by at all. Brody frowned and looked down at the ground.

"Did you ever hear from him?" Gertie asked. "I mean, after he disappeared?"

Brody nodded. "He called right after he left and told me he'd finally gotten the courage to break loose. Said he wasn't looking back. I told him I was happy for him and to keep in touch."

"But he didn't?" Gertie asked.

"No. That was the last I ever heard from him," Brody said. "Until two days ago."

I watched his face closely as he talked. If he was lying, he was doing a good job of it. His voice and expression seemed slightly sad and a little troubled.

"It's a shame Celia came between you two," Gertie said. "If Max had never married her, he might have had an entirely different life. And a longer one."

Brody nodded. "Different perhaps, but probably not much better. Max was always looking for the cool ride and everything that went with it. I think the only thing that would have made him truly happy was having an art career."

I seriously doubted it. After all, it appeared Max had indeed had an art career, and a fairly successful one. But it was also probably what got him killed.

"Anyway," Brody said, "I best get back to it."

"Would you like some help?" Gertie asked.

I mentally shouted "Please say no" over and over again.

Gracie shook her head. "We've only got the front yard left to do. Someone else could probably use your help more. We didn't get much damage. We were lucky." She smiled. "But it was so nice of you to stop by and volunteer. And it was nice to meet you," she said to me.

"It was nice to meet you too," I said and turned to walk away before she could launch into happy land again.

We hopped into my Jeep and pulled away. "Wow," I said. "You weren't kidding with the nice thing. Until she went all *Exorcist* over Celia I was certain she was a Stepford Wife."

"Excellent movie references," Gertie said. "And very accurate choices."

I glanced in my rearview mirror. "Looks like they've shifted from horror to drama."

Gracie's big smile was completely gone and her face was contorted in obvious anger. She was shaking her finger at Brody, who managed to look both aggravated and resigned at the same time.

"I wonder what that's about?" I asked.

"My guess is that Gracie didn't know about Max's phone call to Brody when he disappeared," Ida Belle said.

"What difference does that make?" I asked.

"It doesn't make a difference," Gertie said. "It's just something Brody had that he didn't share with Gracie. She thinks everyone should be an open book, especially when they're married."

"No one is an open book," I said, "and until we can read minds, no one will be."

I meant what I said. I didn't think it was reasonable to think that someone should share their every thought with you, even if you were in a relationship. But the whole scene had struck a nerve. The things I was keeping from Carter were so much bigger than a two-minute conversation with a friend twenty years ago. In reality, almost everything Carter knew about me was a lie, even my appearance.

Ida Belle glanced back at Gertie, but neither of them said anything. They didn't have to. I knew they were both thinking about my own duplicity and how Carter would handle the truth when he finally got it. I was discovering that the downside and the upside of having friends was sometimes the same thing. I couldn't hide things from them anymore. In such a short amount of time, they'd learned my tells...figured me out. Heck, they may know me better than I knew myself.

I sighed. Some days, it wouldn't take much.

"What happened to make Gracie hate Celia so much?" I asked. "It seems out of character with the rest of her."

Ida Belle frowned. "You know, we never figured that out. It was back when they'd all just finished high school. We used to see the four of them running around together—fishing, lunch at the café, road trips to New Orleans—and then one day Gracie was walking down the sidewalk on Main Street and Celia was coming in the opposite direction. I saw Gracie freeze and her face flushed red, then she crossed the street and never looked Celia's direction again."

"And she hasn't ever since," Gertie said, "except to scowl."

"We did some poking around," Ida Belle said. "No good reason except idle curiosity, but it was something odd and you know how we like to figure out odd."

"You like to have all the pieces to the puzzle of Sinful," I said.

"Yes," Ida Belle said. "I suppose we do. At one time, I thought we did, the important ones anyway. Lately, I see how foolish we were to believe we could really know what goes on with people when we're not watching. The irony, of course, being that Gertie, Marge, and I have kept our true selves hidden from the people of Sinful all our lives, but it never occurred to me that other people were doing the same thing."

"You thought this was a simpler place that you could take at face value," I said, "or close to face value, anyway."

"Not face value so much," Ida Belle said. "After all, there's affairs and unexpected pregnancies and addiction problems—all sorts of things people try to keep hidden. But I never figured the people here for the big-ticket items, you know?"

Ida Belle sighed. "It was shortsighted of me. As long as people are involved, the chance of corruption is always present. Sinful is hardly Nirvana. It's certainly not exempt from things that are happening in the rest of the world."

I nodded. "I think a lot of people, even you, would be

surprised at just how much is going on right beneath your nose. Criminals evolve just as any other successful business does. If they weren't getting better at what they do, they wouldn't still be in business."

"Speaking of criminals," Gertie said, "what did you think of Brody as a connection to Randal?"

"He appeared to be telling the truth about Max," I said, "but then, if he's been in contact with Max all these years and living with Gracie, he'd pretty much be an expert at deception. In a lot of ways, Gracie makes the best cover. Who would suspect Brody of being involved in anything bad when he's married to the Pollyanna of Sinful?"

"I agree," Ida Belle said. "Brody is still on the table as a suspect. So where do we go from here?"

"Continue with the canvassing for now," I said. "Gracie's theory that Celia was the target was an interesting one. I want to know what other people think. And I want to know if anyone else talked to Max or saw him talking to anyone else."

"I think we should split up," Ida Belle said. "We can cover more ground that way. Let's pick a block, then you and Gertie can cover one side and I'll cover the other."

I pulled around the corner and stopped at the curb. On both sides of the street, people were working in their yards. "Does this work?" I asked.

"It's as good a place as any," Ida Belle said.

I followed Gertie to the left side of the street and we started working the crowd. We helped move a couple of heavier branches, but mostly people appreciated the offer of help but didn't really need it. Everyone seemed shocked at Max's return and even more so at his murder. No one else shared Gracie's theory that Celia was the intended target, but a few hinted that Celia might have been the shooter.

Toward the end of the street, we saw Belinda Hinkley stacking branches and some shingles at the curb for trash collection. Landon sat on the sidewalk with a young boy, probably ten, looking at a book.

Belinda looked up as we approached. "What brings you out this way?" she asked.

"Since we got lucky with the storm, we're making the rounds," Gertie said. "Seeing if anyone needs help."

"I got lucky as well," Belinda said. "Lost a few shingles and some small branches but nothing hard to fix. My garden is a bit flooded, but since I raised the beds this year, I think everything will be all right."

"That's good," Gertie said. "So far, it seems like everyone has made out okay."

"Everyone but Celia, I suppose," Belinda said.

"Yeah," I said, "I suppose a dead man in your house isn't common hurricane fare."

"Oh, I don't know," Belinda said. "Plenty of people die in a big storm, but most of them weren't murdered."

Since Belinda seemed chatty and clearly had an opinion on things, I figured I'd just come right out and ask. "Who do you think killed him?"

She blinked. "Celia, of course. It's no secret she hated the man, and after that scene at the café, who could blame her? She's been waiting a lot of years to settle the score with Max, and she finally got her chance."

"I suppose you could be right," I said. "He *was* in her house."

Gertie shook her head. "I don't know. Do you really think Celia's capable of killing someone? She's a bitch, but I always saw her as weak at the core. More of a bully who couldn't back it up."

"Under normal circumstances," Belinda said, "I'd agree with you, but these circumstances are far from normal, especially for Celia."

Okay. Clearly the entire thing was outside of the norm. Women's husbands generally didn't disappear without a word and then reappear in a local café decades later as if that were normal. But I got the impression Belinda wasn't talking about Max at all. "What do you mean?" I asked.

"I think Celia was really in love with Max," Belinda said. "I think he may be the only person she's ever loved besides Pansy. Hate is a strong emotion, but it's nothing compared to loving someone. That kind of love can make a person capable of all sorts of things they wouldn't normally be able to do, especially if it turns against you."

I looked over at Gertie, who frowned, apparently considering Belinda's theory. I wasn't certain I believed that completely. I mean, I believed that a person who hated violence could kill to protect themself or someone else, but I couldn't stretch my mind to imagine being so emotionally devastated by a man that I would want to kill him, much less after a twenty-year gap.

I looked at Belinda. "So you're saying that at a certain point, you believe emotion can override character?"

"Not quite that," Belinda said. "I think that strong emotion coupled with the wrong situation can lead to tragedy. For all we know, Max broke into Celia's house to steal something he fancied belonged to him. Between Max's return and that comment he made at the café about Pansy's parentage, Celia's emotions had to be out of control compared to her norm. If she was at home and thought he was an intruder, I think that even once she realized it was Max, she still would have taken the shot."

"So you're saying with her emotions riding high and then confronted with what she thought was a burglar, it might have overwhelmed her to the point that all logic fled?" Gertie asked. "I guess I could see that. Celia's so used to being in charge of everything, but most especially herself. In a compromised mental state, she might have acted out of character."

"But you saw her after she went into her house," I said. "She came back outside and passed out on her porch."

"Maybe she didn't want to believe she'd done it," Gertie said, "and then couldn't face the reality. Remember, she sent Norman to check on her house instead of going herself. Maybe she was hoping it was all a bad dream."

"That's not a compromised mental state," I said. "That's serious delusion."

"I don't pretend to know what happened," Belinda said, "but I stand by my suspicion. If Celia is so innocent, why is she hiding? No one's seen her since she left her house that day."

"Carter knows where she is," I said. "If she's trying to hide from the police, she's not doing a very good job."

"She's hiding from judgment," Belinda said. "Which is futile. It will come soon enough and in a big heap. If you two will excuse me, I have a pot of stew on the stove that I need to check."

She headed inside and I looked over at Gertie. "What do you think about her theory?"

"I think it's an interesting one, and I don't disagree that a compromised mental state could make even the most docile of people a killer."

"But?"

"But it still feels wrong. Maybe it's because I've known Celia all my life, and even though she's a huge pain in the butt, I don't want her to be a murderer. Or maybe I'm just an old fool who still wants to believe that character can't be compromised over something as foolish as a man."

I started across the lawn for the sidewalk. "Do you think Belinda's right about Celia being in love with Max?"

Gertie frowned. "I'd never really given it any thought. Celia's behavior toward things she likes and dislikes has always looked similar to me. She's not a happy person at her core. But I suppose Belinda could be right."

"Which means we might have to change our perspective and put Celia back into the suspect pool."

"Unless Carter has witnesses to clear her."

"Exactly."

"Wanna see my book?" The boy who was sitting with Landon held up a book as we stepped onto the sidewalk next to them.

I looked down and smiled at him, then zeroed in on the book and felt my pulse spike just a hair. "That's a great book," I said. "Can I see?"

He nodded and I took the book from him and looked at the coins, labeled and carefully placed in their respective slots. A history of the origin of the individual coins was contained on each page. I flipped the pages slowly, carefully inspecting the coins until I found one that looked like the dies in Max's apartment.

"This one is really cool," I said and pointed to it.

The boy and Landon leaned over to look. Landon shook his head. "I don't like that one," he said. "I like the one with the horse."

"That one is cool too," I said. "Do you buy the coins?"

"I don't buy them," the boy said, "'cause I'm only eight and my allowance is only two dollars a week. Mostly people give them to me for birthdays and stuff. Mr. Sampson gave me the one you like."

I glanced over at Gertie, who raised her eyebrows. "Does Mr. Sampson collect coins too?" I asked.

The boy shrugged. "I guess so, but they weren't in a book or anything. He just had a big bag of them."

"That was very nice of him to share," I said. "Has Mr. Sampson given you any other coins?"

"No. That was the only one." The boy's eyes widened and his hand flew up to cover his mouth. "I wasn't supposed to tell where I got it. Mr. Sampson made me promise."

"Don't worry," I said and handed him the book. "Your secret is safe with us."

The boy looked relieved. "Good, because I don't want Mr. Sampson mad at me. He might have another bag of coins sometime, and if he knew I told, he probably wouldn't give me one."

We started across the street where Ida Belle was standing at the curb. "You get anything?" I asked.

Ida Belle nodded. "Two people saw Max talking to Brody on Main Street, and their account of the length of the conversation was a lot different than Brody's. More like ten minutes and not two, and both of them said Brody looked mad. What about you guys?"

"We found a coin like the dies in Max's apartment," Gertie said.

"Found it where?" Ida Belle asked.

I recounted our conversation with Belinda and then with the boy. "Who was the kid, anyway?" I asked.

"The Dugas boy," Gertie said. "The youngest one. I think his name is Ian."

Ida Belle glanced across the street. "That's Ian. Any idea how much that coin is worth?"

I pulled out my phone and did a search. "Looks like they're worth about five hundred apiece. The real ones, anyway."

"And Brody just handed over one to Ian and no one questioned it?"

I scrolled down on my phone. "Apparently there was a fire at some mint and a bunch of the coins were destroyed, which increased the value of those remaining. It was worth about fifty bucks before last year. The other coins in the book were the cheaper collectibles, so it probably wouldn't occur to anyone to think the boy had been given something really valuable."

"Especially if he never told them," Gertie said.

"And he may not have," I said. "He said different people gave him coins. Unless his parents were paying close attention to each gift coin, they probably don't know what he has and doesn't have or where they came from."

"Probably not," Ida Belle agreed. "So this puts a new spin on Brody."

"Definitely," I said. "So do we keep going?"

Ida Belle looked up at the sky. "We've got another three hours or so of daylight. I say we keep at it until then. We may find out more."

"I'd like to find someone who saw Max that night," I said. "Especially if it helped narrow down time of death."

"Carter may have found someone," Gertie said. "Any decent person would have reported seeing Max to the sheriff's department as soon as they heard what happened."

"Yeah, but what good does that do us?" I asked. "Carter's not going to give us details about an open investigation."

"You could try that feminine wiles thing," Gertie said. "I have faith in you."

"You do not. You just want to see me embarrass myself."

Her guilty look gave her away.

"Let's get on with it," I said.

I didn't want to admit that their lack of confidence in my female abilities bothered me just a little. I knew I needed work on girlie things. Director Morrow was always exasperated when I came close to blowing cover because I knew how to be an operative way better than how to be female. But I must be getting better at it. After all, Carter was into me, and it's not like he was hard up. All of the single women in Sinful and at least half of the married ones still looked at his butt when he walked away.

Maybe after we were done canvassing the neighborhood, I'd take a shower, put on one of those cute short sundresses, and head down to the sheriff's department just to prove them wrong.

Chapter Thirteen

I cut a huge hunk of meat loaf and put it on a tray next to a heaping pile of mashed potatoes and two long slices of French bread. "Can I have a piece of that pie?" I asked Ally and pointed to the chocolate pie she'd taken out of the oven about ten minutes before.

"Sure," she said. "It should be cool enough to cut by now. Are you taking Carter some dinner?"

"Yeah. He finally went home to grab some sleep this morning, but he's going to man the sheriff's department until midnight. Deputy Breaux was done in, so he sent him home."

"Who's going to work dispatch?"

"Carter got Myrtle back. She's going on shift at midnight."

"Really? How did that happen?"

Myrtle had been the sheriff department's dispatcher, receptionist, administrative assistant, and more importantly, Ida Belle and Gertie's inside informant forever, but when Celia was elected mayor and replaced Sheriff Lee with her cousin Nelson, the first thing he'd done was let Myrtle go and replace her with his hooker girlfriend. Now that Sinful was rid of Nelson and his hooker, the dispatcher position was vacant.

"I don't know for sure," I said, "but my guess is he called her up and said 'come back to work.'"

"I hope she sprays down that chair with Lysol. That *thing* Nelson had in there was seriously gross."

"I think Carter burned it," I said. "Anyway, I guess with Celia hiding out like a criminal, she's not likely to come raise hell about the sheriff's department employees."

"I'm sure you're right. I think Carter is well past asking permission to do much of anything, and I can't say that I blame him. Aunt Celia has single-handedly reduced the safety in this town simply by being herself."

"I agree, but you'd never get her to admit that."

"Of course not." Ally cut a slice of the pie and put it in a container, then handed it to me. "You look pretty. Between you and the food, Carter's day should get a lot better."

"You think I look okay?" I glanced at my reflection in the toaster. The turquoise sundress matched the color of my eyes, and up next to my tanned skin and pink lip gloss, my eyes and the dress seemed even more vibrant. My hair, which was usually in a convenient ponytail, was blow-dried straight, and the golden locks hung past my shoulders, as smooth and shiny as silk.

"No," Ally said. "You don't look okay. You look awesome. Stop fishing for compliments and get that food to your man."

She gave me a shove and I grabbed the two food containers and my Jeep keys and headed out. I hadn't been fishing for compliments. I wasn't even certain I could. I'd seen plenty of women do it before and it always seemed awkward and somewhat embarrassing. And it wasn't like I didn't know what pretty looked like. I saw pretty women all the time on television and in person. Ally was pretty, and when Francine was younger, I would bet she was smoking hot.

But it was still hard to see it in myself, even though the more I saw myself decked out like this, the more I saw my mother in me. And everyone thought my mother was beautiful. I thought she was the most beautiful woman in the world, but then I also lost her way too young.

I made the drive into Sinful and unloaded my wares, then headed into the sheriff's department. Carter was at the front desk working on his laptop when I walked in. He looked up at me and his eyes widened, then he smiled. "This is a nice surprise."

"Are you sure?" I asked and slid the food onto his desk. "I hope I'm not interrupting. I know you've been slammed and running on a couple hours' sleep."

He leaned forward and sniffed. "Is that Ally's meat loaf?"

"You know it. We're still whittling down Gertie's red meat supply. I've also got mashed potatoes and chocolate pie."

"Will you and Ally marry me?"

I laughed. "I don't think you can handle both of us."

"Baby, I can't handle you." He rose from the desk and came around to stand in front of me, then cupped my face with his hands. He lowered his lips to mine and my skin started to tingle. I slid my arms around him and moved closer until our bodies were pressing against each other.

He deepened the kiss and I ran my arms down his back, mentally admiring his tone. Carter LeBlanc was all male and a prime specimen. I couldn't help but wonder what he looked like naked. I bet it was a sight to behold. I only hoped that once the truth came out, I still had the opportunity.

He broke off the kiss and smiled. "That was even better than the food."

"How can you be certain? You haven't tried the food yet."

"Manna from heaven couldn't compete with your lips and cherry lip gloss."

I felt a blush creep up my neck. No matter how many times Carter complimented me, it still made me feel squishy all over. I'd had men attracted to me before and they'd definitely laid the flattery on thick, but when Carter said things, it felt as though he really meant them. It didn't feel like a cheap come-on.

As he moved back behind the desk, he pulled a chair over next to him. "Sit with me while I eat," he said. "If you have time, that is."

"I have plenty of time," I said as I slid onto the chair. "Ally and I finished dinner already and she's off on a baking spree. Ida Belle and Gertie are coming over later for movie night, and that's all I've got going on."

I didn't tell the part where they were currently over at the General Store to see what they could get out of Walter, or that after the movie, they'd be bunking at my place. Ally wasn't in on anything either, and that's the way we intended to keep it. As far as everyone else was concerned, we would stay up too late and drink too much, then all crash.

Carter uncovered the tray that contained the meat loaf and stabbed a big hunk of meat with a plastic fork. He popped it in his mouth and closed his eyes. "That is awesome," he said after he swallowed. "You know, if Ally ever opened her own restaurant, I think she could give Francine a run for her money."

"I don't doubt it, but I don't think she wants the responsibility of a restaurant. It's got to be a ton of work. Speaking of which, how's everything going down here? Have things settled down yet?"

He nodded. "All the missing husbands are accounted for. They're broke this time because they spent all night in a casino in New Orleans, but I'm not about to tell their wives that."

"I don't blame you."

"Nobody sustained any major damage. Some of the homes farther out still don't have power, but that's nothing new. They all have backup plans for this sort of thing. The storm didn't last long enough for the vandalism or burglaries to get out of hand, the missing cats have all wandered home, so I'd say it's pretty much back to normal."

"Except for Max's murder."

"Yeah, except for that."

"Did you ever talk to Celia, or does she still think she's invisible?"

He scowled. "That woman makes me want to take a permanent vacation. It's no wonder Max vanished from here. It was probably the only way he could escape."

"I take it the conversation didn't go well."

"That's an understatement. Do you know what she had the nerve to suggest?"

"That Marie killed Max and she did it in Celia's house to frame her for it so that Marie could get the mayor's position?"

Carter stared at me and blinked. "Yeah. How did you know?"

"After she accused me of doing it, Ida Belle popped off that theory. I figured if you questioned her, she'd throw out that crazy train to try to direct things away from herself. You don't give that ridiculous theory any credence, right?"

"Please. Even if I didn't think Celia was insane most of the time, not to mention walking around with a persecution complex of monumental proportion, Marie has an ironclad alibi."

"Please tell me it's for the whole night?"

"The time of death range isn't quite that big, but the answer is still yes. She was bunking at the Olsen house with two other families. The Olsens have this enormous kitchen and family room area. Everyone stayed in that one room the entire night. Several of the adults and a couple of the kids stayed up all night, and they all insisted Marie never left the room except to use the bathroom."

"Was she in there for long?" I asked. If I knew Celia, she'd still push to make a case even if there was only a five-minute window to work with.

"She could have been in there for an hour. The bathroom is a half bath located right off the living room and it's an interior room. So unless Marie went into the half bath, teleported to Celia's house, then shot Max and teleported back, there's absolutely no way she could have been the shooter."

"Good. Then there's no way Celia can make trouble for Marie."

"Oh, she's still trying. She told me that unless I arrested Marie, she would appoint a new sheriff tomorrow and have me fired."

"For Christ's sake. Does that woman's ego have an end?"

"Not that I can see."

"What did you tell her?"

"Okay."

I blinked. "You said you'd arrest Marie?"

"Why not? I called up Marie, told her the score, and asked if I could pick her up and bring her down to the sheriff's department for an hour or so. Then I called the DA and told him what was up. He told me to get Marie back home before she filed a lawsuit against the department."

I laughed. "Oh my God. That's classic. Celia may still have some control over the sheriff's department, but the DA doesn't have to bow down to any of her nonsense."

"Exactly. It helps that the DA knows Celia personally. His mother's family is from Sinful and he grew up visiting. He's heard enough stories to know the score. He said any time she pulls that crap to simply arrest someone and give him a call."

"That is brilliant. I would have paid money to see the look on Celia's face when you told her what the DA said."

"Oh, it gets even better." Carter grinned. "When she got all pissy about the DA, I told her that her next order might not be easy to make as she'd be sitting in the sheriff's department jail."

"You told Celia you were going to arrest her? She must have had kittens."

"She turned forty shades of red and her chest swelled up like a moose. I thought she was going to explode."

"Wait. Why would she think you would arrest her?" Carter's story, while amusing, suddenly didn't make sense.

Carter's smile faded as he realized he'd just stepped into confidential investigative territory. The thing with Marie we would no doubt hear from Marie, but the other wasn't street gossip.

I stared at him for a moment and then it clicked. "Celia doesn't have an alibi."

Carter pretended to focus on his dinner and I knew I was right.

"Holy crap! That is awesome. I know you can't say anything, or won't, whatever, but you just got handed a get out of jail free card. Or in this case, a keep running the jail free card."

"Hmmm," Carter said and stabbed another piece of meat loaf.

I narrowed my eyes at him. "You don't actually think she did it, do you?"

He gave me an "are you kidding" glare.

I held my hands up. "Sorry. I should have known. Hey, I know you can't tell me anything, but that doesn't work two ways. So do you want to hear something I heard today that made me wonder about things for a minute?"

"All one-way-street conversations are both legal and often interesting, especially given the company you three tend to keep."

"We were keeping regular Sinful company today. Since we didn't have serious damage, we drove around, seeing if other people needed help."

Carter narrowed his eyes. "Just being altruistic? I'm not buying that for a minute. So what gossip did you pick up?"

"Nothing of merit, really. Everyone seems surprised by Max's return and even more so by his murder, but Gracie Sampson had an interesting suggestion. She suggested that Celia was the intended target, not Max."

Carter considered this for a moment, then shrugged. "I suppose it works on some level. It was Celia's house, and with the storm and the power outage, someone could have mistaken a silhouette in the dark for Celia rather than Max."

I nodded. "That's why I found it interesting. On the surface, it makes sense."

"But not when you shift to motive. I'm well aware that Celia has her enemies, and I'm positive that all of them would like to see her thrown out of office and maybe even run out of town, but that's where it ends."

"That's basically what I said—that the gap between hating someone and killing them was still a really wide one. But Gracie seems dedicated to the thought."

"Probably wishful thinking," he said. "There's some old feud between Gracie and Celia. I've asked my mom about it before, but she didn't know what the falling-out was about. Just that it was a long time ago and hasn't lessened."

"Maybe Gracie is part Italian. She certainly seems to have that grudge thing down, especially for someone walking around with a smile painted on her face."

He laughed. "Yeah, a little bit of Gracie goes a long way."

"A little bit of Gracie could make you diabetic. All that saccharine sweetness. I needed to brush my teeth afterward."

"I can see that." He sobered for a moment and seemed contemplative. He was silent for so long, I started to worry just a little. Had he heard something about our trip to New Orleans? I didn't see how he could have, but one never knew who might have a cousin or something who heard something and reported back.

"I was thinking," he said. "When all this is cleared up, maybe you and I could take a weekend trip to New Orleans. See the city for a couple days, eat some good food, maybe throw some money away at the casino…"

I felt my heart leap in my throat, and other parts of me started to tingle. What Carter was suggesting was huge. It would take our relationship to a whole new level—the level I'd sorta been avoiding because of emotional stuff but secretly dying for because of physical stuff. My heart and body wanted me to yell "hell, yes" and pack a bag. My head was shouting "not until you tell him the truth."

Apparently, I hesitated too long, because Carter said, "Never mind. It was a stupid suggestion."

"No," I said quickly. "It wasn't stupid at all. I was just surprised. It's been a long time since…" Like forever. I'd never gone away for a long weekend with a man. I'd dated—at least I guess you could call it that—but I'd never been with anyone that I would consider sharing living space with for any length of time.

Carter's expression shifted from offended to sympathetic. "It's been a long time for me too. I guess I subconsciously swore off relationships. I didn't realize it, really. Not until you came along."

"Mine was more of a conscious decision. That's why I'm so careful. I didn't really plan on this, and with me being here only for the summer…"

And with me being a CIA assassin, and here under a false identity, and not being at all the person you think I am.

Carter frowned. "It's not logical, given the situation, and you can bet that's something I've thought about at length. But ultimately, I can't deny my attraction to you. You're the most interesting woman I've ever known."

"Interesting? Is that what you're calling it these days? I thought I was a Yankee imported terror."

He laughed. "I admit that a lot of your choices frustrate the heck out of me, but that doesn't make them not interesting. In fact, because you seem hell-bent on doing exactly what you want and everyone else be damned, it might make you even more attractive."

I blushed and stared down at the desk, wondering what Carter would think about the real me. Would he find that person interesting, or would he be appalled? Sure, Carter had been a soldier, and even though we'd never talked much about his time overseas, I was sure he'd seen and done things that civilians would never understand. But my profession took soldiering to an entirely different level. It required a disassociation from humanity that most people weren't capable of understanding, much less achieving.

"A weekend trip sounds like a lot of fun," I said finally. What the hell. It wasn't a lie. It did sound like a lot of fun, and maybe the CIA and FBI setup would bag Ahmad and all of this could be over. My confession would probably be a lot less harsh if people weren't still trying to kill me.

Carter smiled and I could see the tension leave his shoulders. Unfortunately, it had settled right into mine. Despite all my good intentions, I was digging a deeper and deeper hole.

My phone buzzed. My hand clenched when I saw the message from Gertie.

The alarm is going off at my house. I told the alarm company to shut it off and figured we'd go check it out, but Ida Belle said to let Carter handle it. She's an old poop. If you go with him, will you please get my good blue lawn chair out of the shed?

I frowned.

"Is something wrong?" Carter asked.

"Gertie's at my house and her house alarm went off."

"She still has that thing? I thought she'd taken an ax to it after the false alarms."

"I think this thing with Max bothers her more than she'll admit," I said. "Lately, Sinful hasn't exactly been the sleepy town it used to be."

"That's true enough." Carter rose from his chair. "I guess I better go check it out."

"Is it okay if I come with you? Gertie wants me to grab a chair from her shed."

"Given that it's probably the alarm on the fritz or operator error, I suppose it wouldn't hurt. Besides, if I don't, you'll just go afterward and get the chair."

"You know me too well."

I followed Carter out of the sheriff's department and hopped into his truck. With any luck, the alarm was as faulty as Gertie claimed and this would amount to a whole lot of nothing. But I wasn't convinced enough to ignore it, and I didn't want Carter going in blind. If the men in New Orleans had tracked Gertie down by her license plate, they could have shown up at her house.

Gertie's house looked fine when we pulled up to the curb. In anticipation of being at my house, Gertie had left the porch light on, but that was the only thing that looked different than it usually did. "Everything looks normal," I said.

Carter nodded as we walked up the sidewalk to the house. He checked the front door and it was still locked. A quick review of the windows showed them to be secure as well.

"I'll look around back while you get the chair," Carter said.

We headed through the gate and into the backyard. Carter

started with the windows and I set off across the lawn for the shed that was tucked in the back corner. I was almost there when I heard Carter yell.

"There's a broken window back here."

I started to turn around, but then I heard a noise in the bushes in front of me. A second later, a man with an assault rifle burst out of the bush and leveled his gun at me.

Chapter Fourteen

Without even thinking, I lunged forward, grabbing the barrel of the rifle with my right hand, pushing it away from me then pulling it toward me and down at the same time. When the shooter stepped forward, off balance, I struck him in the nose with my left hand, then reached down to grab the stock of the rifle. With my right hand still grasping the barrel, I shoved the gun upward, clocking him in the forehead. As I took one step back, I pulled the gun down and backward, breaking his grasp, then flipped it over and fired a single shot into his heart.

The entire event took only seconds to play out, but it felt as if everything were in slow motion. I stood there staring down at the man. I could hear the faint sound of footsteps pounding behind me as my pulse throbbed in my temples. A second man bolted from behind the shed and before I could even lift the rifle, a shot fired behind me, hitting him square in the middle of the head. He dropped like a stone. I stood there, my heart pounding so hard my chest hurt.

This wasn't the guys from the alley. These men worked for Ahmad.

Carter checked the two men for a pulse and removed the remaining weapons from their bodies. He glanced back at me several times, but was completely silent as he worked. When he'd collected the small arsenal and placed it in a pile behind me, he stepped in front of me.

His expression was a mixture of anger, frustration, and disappointment. "If I run your prints, what will I see?" he asked quietly.

I dropped my gaze to the ground, unable to look him eye to eye. "You'll see information on Sandy-Sue Morrow."

He sighed. "What agency?"

Carter knew the score. Not just anyone could attach one person's fingerprints to another person's existence. It took someone with federal placement and high up the food chain.

I looked back up at him. "CIA."

"And the real Sandy-Sue Morrow?"

"Is vacationing in Europe, courtesy of my boss who happens to be her uncle."

His expression darkened. "Gerald Morrow is your boss?"

Crap. "Yeah. You know him?"

"I worked with some of his men in Iraq." His voice was steady when he delivered the sentence, but I saw the tiny shift in his eyes.

If Carter had worked with Morrow's operatives in Iraq, then he knew exactly what I was. Morrow dealt with only one type of operative.

"I'm sorry I didn't tell you the truth," I said.

"No you're not. You're just sorry I found out before the summer was over and you could disappear."

"No! That's not it at all." I struggled to find the words that could explain everything I'd felt and thought and agonized over since I'd realized my feelings for Carter went deeper than I ever expected.

"I couldn't tell you the truth," I said. "I couldn't compromise my identity or put you at risk. I was going to tell you the truth before I left. I just needed things settled." I sighed. "I shouldn't have gotten involved with you at all."

"That's probably the only thing you're sorry for."

My heart clenched and my stomach rolled. I felt tears well up in my eyes, and I struggled to keep them from falling. "Not in the way you're implying."

But I knew my words were just that—words.

Carter hated me, and I didn't blame him. I had lied to him about everything from the moment we'd first met and continued the lie even after I'd gotten personally involved with him. What I'd done was understandable on a professional basis, but inexcusable on a personal one.

"You know," he said, "I'm angrier at myself than anything. I knew you didn't add up—all that poking your nose into criminal activity, your knowledge of certain things that was well beyond the average civilian, that dive you made to drag me from the bottom of the lake—but I didn't want to believe it, so I stuck my head in the sand. It was stupid, but it's all on me."

"No, it's not. You weren't supposed to know. You can't blame yourself."

"Do Ida Belle and Gertie know? Ally?"

I felt my heart drop into my stomach all over again.

"Ida Belle and Gertie do. Ally doesn't know anything."

His face flushed red. "I see. So you could tell two nosy old ladies, but you couldn't tell the man you were in a relationship with?"

"They're not...I didn't..." What the hell could I say to explain why Gertie and Ida Belle knew without giving away their secret? "I didn't tell them. Shortly after I arrived, they saw me do something, just like you did. Something they recognized from their time in the service."

He narrowed his eyes at me. "That situation at Gertie's house, right after you arrived. It wasn't Gertie and Ida Belle who took them, was it?"

"I don't know anything about that." It was the biggest lie in the world, and I was sure Carter knew I was lying. I was also sure he understood why I couldn't tell the truth. The last thing I could afford was being implicated in a crime, even if I was the person who'd ended someone else's crime spree.

"Of course you don't." He waved his hand at the bodies. "Do you know anything about these men? Or is that something else you're going to pretend ignorance on?"

I shook my head. Director Morrow wasn't going to like it, but at this point it would be irresponsible and dangerous to leave Carter in the dark. I wasn't interested in either.

"They work for Ahmad, an arms dealer in the Middle East. I was undercover in his organization when I got made. Director Morrow is certain there's a leak at the CIA that compromised my cover, and after I blew cover Ahmad put a price on my head."

"Which is why you're not in protective custody." Carter blew out a breath. "How do you think they found you?"

"I'm not sure that they did." I gave him a brief rundown of everything that had happened since the counterfeit money blew through Sinful.

When I was finished, Carter stared at me for several seconds, his expression a mixture of frustration and a tiny bit of disbelief. I didn't blame him. It was a huge coincidence.

"Wait," he said finally. "You said these weren't the guys from the alley behind the art gallery."

"They're not."

"Then why would they be here at Gertie's house?"

"I think they might have followed the guys from the alley here."

"Why would you make that leap?"

I pointed to the hedges. "Because I think the men from the alley had already been dispatched before we arrived."

Carter turned around to look at the hedges where I pointed to the tip of a shoe sticking out from under the bush. He walked over and pushed branches of the bushes aside and peered inside. I knew the men from the alley were both in the bushes as soon as he turned around.

"This is a huge mess," he said. "I don't even know how to report it, but I can't leave four bodies in Gertie's backyard and I can't just send them to the morgue without paperwork." He ran one hand through his hair. "Jesus H. Christ!"

He was right. It was a huge problem, and I didn't have a clue how to handle it.

"Carter?" Deputy Breaux's voice sounded behind us and I jumped. "Is everything all right? Mr. Templeton called about gunshots and said he couldn't reach anyone down at the sheriff's department."

Carter looked at me, and I could see the panic on his face. He didn't just have to come up with an explanation that worked, he had to do it in a matter of seconds. "No, Deputy Breaux. We have a situation here."

"What kind of situ—oh, Christ! That's a body. That's two bodies. What in the world happened?"

"I'm not entirely sure," Carter said. "Gertie's house alarm went off, but it's always been broken so I didn't think much of it. Fortune had dropped me some dinner by the department and rode with me to pick up a chair Gertie requested she get from her shed."

"And you found them like this?" Deputy Breaux asked.

Carter shook his head. "When we went to get the chair, one of them came out of the bushes with an assault rifle. I managed to disarm him and got off a clean shot, then the second man came around the shed and I took him out with my service revolver."

Deputy Breaux's eyes widened with fear and admiration. "Wow! That is something else. I wish I would have seen it. So what were they doing in Gertie's backyard?"

"I don't know for certain, but I suspect they killed the two men hidden in Gertie's bushes."

Deputy Breaux's head jerked around to stare at the bushes. "There's two more bodies in there. Holy crap. That's more dead people than I've ever seen in one place, even the funeral home."

"It's practically an infestation," I said.

Deputy Breaux looked over at me. "Are you all right? I can't imagine how scary that was being right in the middle of it."

"I'm fine," I said.

"She's a lot tougher than she looks," Carter said. "Can you call and get a pickup of these bodies for me? I've got the camera in my truck. I just need to document the scene. I'll do the paperwork when I get back to the department."

Deputy Breaux nodded and looked over at me. "Do you need me to give you a ride? I don't think you should stay here with the bodies and all."

I looked over at Carter, desperately wanting him to say I had to stay and give my statement. Maybe then I'd have a better chance to explain. After I'd had a chance to process it all and not while I was standing over a man I'd just killed.

"Go ahead," Carter said. "I can take your statement tomorrow."

His tone was so dismissive that I felt the tears well up all over again. He bent over one of the bodies and pretended to check it, but I knew it was his way of avoiding looking at me. I turned around and followed Deputy Breaux out of the back lawn, perched on the edge of completely losing my composure.

I'd thought my life was over when I got sent to Sinful. If I'd known it was just beginning, I would have done things a lot differently.

Chapter Fifteen

Ida Belle and Gertie were sitting in my living room when I walked in the front door. They barely looked up when I walked inside, their eyes glued to the television.

"Francine had a baking emergency that Ally went to tend to," Gertie said. "I sent you a million texts, but I guess you were busy with more important things." She elbowed Ida Belle.

I walked into the living room like a zombie and sank into the first chair. They looked at each other, instantly sobering.

"What happened?" Ida Belle asked.

The dam burst. All the tears that I'd been holding back came flooding out. Tears for hurting Carter with my lies. Tears for ruining my career because I refused to follow protocol. Tears for my mother whom I missed so much and tears for a father I didn't miss at all. Tears because I hadn't realized just how much everything in Sinful mattered until I was faced with losing it.

Gertie and Ida Belle jumped up from the couch and hurried over. Gertie leaned over and put her arm around my shoulders. Ida Belle sat on the coffee table and put her hand on my arm.

"Whatever it is, we can fix it," Gertie said, but her voice was laced more with fear rather than conviction. My breakdown had scared and surprised them.

"Not this time," I sobbed. "Everything is ruined."

"You told Carter the truth," Ida Belle said.

I nodded and wiped my eyes with the back of my hand. "I

had no choice. He made me just like you two did."

Gertie sucked in a breath. "The men were at my house?"

"Yeah, but they were already dead. Ahmad's men had taken them out. They hid behind the shed when we arrived. I just...reacted, you know? The first one rushed me from the bushes, holding an assault rifle, and I dispatched him like he was a pizza delivery boy."

"You killed him?" Ida Belle asked.

I nodded. "I disarmed him and shot him with his own weapon. The entire exchange probably took three seconds. I was standing there in shock from the dispatch when the second one ran out and Carter shot him."

"Disarming and disabling men with assault rifles isn't exactly the kind of thing librarians are known for," Gertie said. "I take it the revelation wasn't well received."

"That's the biggest understatement I've heard since I've been in Sinful," I said.

"I'm so sorry," Gertie said. "Give him some time. This was a shock, I'm sure."

"How could it not be?" Ida Belle agreed. "Not only is Carter hurt on an emotional level, his pride has taken a huge hit. You fooled him, and he's not easily fooled."

Everything they said was absolutely true. I knew Carter had been shocked, then angry, and at some point almost resigned. I knew I'd hurt him on every level possible except physical, although I had just discovered that severe emotional pain caused you physical pain. Every muscle in my body was knotted. My stomach felt as if I'd eaten bad Chinese food. My head pounded as though I'd been struck with a two-by-four. Getting shot hurt less.

"I didn't just injure his pride," I said. "I decimated it. He asked me if you two knew."

"Oh no." Gertie's hand flew up to cover her mouth.

"And you had to tell him we did," Ida Belle said. "At this point, it couldn't be helped. Nothing that's happened since you arrived in Sinful makes sense unless we were in on it from the beginning. It won't take Carter long to piece everything together. Everything he only had a mild suspicion of before, he'll know he was right about."

"And he'll know things couldn't have happened that way unless we knew," Gertie said. "We wouldn't place that kind of trust in someone if they couldn't back it up, and we wouldn't have taken part if we hadn't been qualified to do so ourselves." Gertie looked over at Ida Belle and sighed. "We had a good run, sister."

I looked at Gertie, confused. "Wait—I didn't tell Carter about you guys."

They both frowned.

"But how did you explain telling us and not telling him?" Gertie asked.

"I told him you made me right after I arrived, just like he did. That you recognized the moves from your time in Vietnam and knew no civilian could have pulled them off."

Ida Belle looked at Gertie, then back at me. "We appreciate your loyalty, Fortune, and we understand you live by a soldier's code, but this isn't a bullet we want you to take. If Carter knew the truth about us, it might make him feel better about not connecting the dots with you before now."

Gertie nodded. "Right now, it looks to him like two old ladies got the jump on him."

I shook my head. "I won't blow a soldier's cover. Ever. If you want to tell him the truth, that's up to you, but he'll never hear a word of your past from me. I made you a promise, and that's worth more to me than my broken heart or Carter's pride."

Gertie gave my shoulders a squeeze. "They don't make them like you anymore."

I felt tears well up again as the entire last hour replayed in my mind.

"Maybe that's a good thing," I said as I dissolved into tears once more.

Between crying jags, wallowing and two hot showers, I took up an hour and a half of the night. The only lucky break I got was when Ally called to say she'd be working with Francine well into the night and was going to bunk with her. At least it bought me some time to come up with a cover story for the end of my relationship with Carter. I couldn't exactly tell the truth, and Sinful residents would be on that change in wind direction like stink on crap.

The call from the sheriff's department came as I'd just stepped out of the shower for the second time. Carter needed to get statements from all of us, and he wanted to talk to Gertie first as it was her house.

"I'm not ready to face him," I said, still wrapped in a towel and running a comb through my hair.

"Of course you're not," Gertie said, "but you don't have a choice."

"You think I don't know that?" I tossed the comb in the sink. "There are four dead men in the morgue and I killed one of them. More importantly, they would have killed you if they'd found you at home. The man I dispatched didn't hesitate. He was going to kill whoever was in your backyard, whether they were a threat or not."

They both stood there silently watching me, probably waiting for me to either explode or start crying again. I felt like doing both, but I wasn't going to do either. I was done being a regular girl. It was time to become a soldier again.

"Look," I said, "I know something has to be done. I wouldn't have ever come to Sinful if the threat wasn't real. I know better than anyone the level of evil we're dealing with. You two take my Jeep and go on ahead. I'm going to call Harrison and bring him up to speed. I should have as soon as it happened."

"Do you think you'll be in trouble?" Gertie asked.

"I'm going to be in so much trouble, I probably won't see anything but a desk for at least a decade. That's if I get to keep my job at all."

"I'm so sorry," Gertie said, her dismay obvious. "We should have never asked you to take the risks that we did. It's our fault you're in this mess."

"Don't even go there. It's *all* my fault. I've always had a problem following orders, which is how I wound up here in the first place. I've always pushed it. Always had something to prove. If this time it costs me everything, then I only have myself to blame."

And that was the bottom line. I could rage at my mother for dying and leaving me when I needed her the most. I could rage at my father for barely showing a passing interest in his only child. I could blame society for expecting women to be less capable in certain jobs than men. I could blame the CIA for the rules that tied agents' hands so often.

But what difference did it make?

It was a bunch of explanations but not an excuse. The bottom line is that no matter why I did the things I did, I always had a choice in doing them.

"You're sure you'll be okay here by yourself?" Gertie asked.

I smiled. "Everyone is probably safer if I'm alone."

Ida Belle nodded. "I'll text you when we're done, then we'll come get you for your round."

"What are you going to tell Carter when he asks why I'm not there?" I asked.

"I'll tell him you're taking care of business," Ida Belle said. "He can deal with it or not. Despite my empathy for his broken heart situation, we've got a much bigger problem to address."

"Thanks," I said. I watched as they made their way out of my bedroom and then looked out the window as they stopped in front of my Jeep and had a brief argument. I smiled. Gertie wanted to drive and Ida Belle was refusing. Ida Belle climbed into the driver's seat and Gertie flopped into the passenger's seat, still wearing a pout as they drove away.

It was nice when some things were always the same. It made life feel secure, even though I knew better than most people that security was as big a myth as control.

I put on yoga pants, T-shirt, and tennis shoes, then pulled my hair back into a ponytail. No sundresses. No lip gloss. No shiny wave of fake hair running across my shoulders. Those days were over.

I went downstairs and grabbed my cell phone. I took a deep breath and slowly blew it out before dialing Harrison's number. This was not going to be a pleasant conversation. Part of me hoped I got his voice mail and could put it off just a little longer, but as my luck was running, he answered on the first ring.

"It's me," I said. "I have a big problem."

"Shit."

Usually when I called Harrison with an issue, I always described it as a "little problem." The fact that I was coming out and stating this was a big one left him no doubt that I was about to dump a huge mess on him.

I gave him a rundown on everything that had happened,

starting with my unauthorized investigation of Max's apartment in New Orleans and ending with my dispatch of one of Ahmad's men. When I finished, there was dead silence on the other end of the phone. It lasted so long that I thought for a moment Harrison had either had a heart attack or simply left his phone on the coffee table, formed a new identity, and fled the country. I wouldn't blame him if he did. Partnering with me couldn't be easy.

Then the explosion came.

A good two minutes of cursing and yelling—some of the words and phrases were things I'd never even heard. I was pretty sure he was so angry he was making stuff up. Finally, he ran out of either creativity or air and he went silent.

"I've got to go down to the sheriff's department to make a statement here shortly," I said. "I need to know how to proceed."

"You said the deputy took responsibility for the shot, right? Is he going to go on record with that?"

"I think so. No one would think twice about it if he did it, whereas if he put on the record that I did…well, it would blow my cover and make him look foolish given that we were sorta dating and he had no idea who I really was."

Harrison blew out a breath. "You know, you have had some real doozies before, but this one takes the cake. I bet we could drop you off on a deserted island and you'd still find a way to screw things up."

"Probably."

The resignation and exhaustion I felt must have come through in that single word, because Harrison backed off of me and shifted back to the job.

"So Ahmad's men killed Randal's men. Is that right?"

"I can't be positive they were Randal's men, but that's what

I think. The other two were definitely Ahmad's. I recognized one of them."

"Did they recognize you?"

"I don't think so. I didn't see a flicker of recognition in the one I dispatched, but then he didn't have time to focus on my looks either. I didn't get a good look at the other man before Carter fired. I think Randal's men tracked Gertie's license plate and got her home address. My guess is Ahmad's men followed them thinking they'd get a line on the counterfeiter."

"It doesn't matter. It puts them all dangerously close to you. And what if the one hiding behind the shed sent a text telling Ahmad that he'd seen you? He had time before he ran out to do it?"

I felt my stomach clench a little. "Carter searched them. I'm sure if he found anything that indicated my cover was blown, he would have contacted me right away."

"Yeah, probably so, but still, it's too close for comfort. You've been hanging out with those old ladies since you arrived. It wouldn't take someone a lot of time to track them back to you. Randal's men got a good look at you at the apartment. Even if the guys in the alley are dead, I'm sure they reported in with a description."

"True."

"You should have contacted me when you got the information on Randal."

"It was just a theory," I said. "We wanted to make the connection, but yes, you're right. I should have given you the name as soon as I suspected he was Jamison's counterfeit connection."

"Well, no sense harping on it now, but with Randal's and Ahmad's guys dead, it's not going to take long for both camps to come out swinging with the front line and burying evidence with the back one."

It was all things I'd already processed, and they were no less grim with Harrison laying them out verbally as I'd already done mentally.

"So how do we proceed?" I asked.

"First, I get the three of you out of Sinful. Normally, I'd pull you out altogether and send the old ladies to the Bahamas, but I think the things they know might be beneficial to the investigation, and God help me for saying this, but I don't trust pulling off the takedown without you. The FBI has some great agents, but no one is more qualified for this than you."

It was the only time I remembered Harrison extending me a compliment. I knew he appreciated my skills, as I did his. We'd saved each other's lives enough times to have a deep respect for each other when it came to the work. But he'd never actually come out and said I was better at something than others. Under ordinary circumstances, it would have been a real ego boost, but now, I almost wished it weren't true.

If I weren't so skilled, so devoted, so tunnel-visioned, maybe my life wouldn't be falling apart.

"Okay," I said. "You secure the safe house and then let me know how passage will be handled. I'll let Ida Belle and Gertie know we're relocating."

"And your deputy friend. He's not going to be happy about the CIA yanking you out from under him. He'll be even madder if you disappear without telling him. Just no information on the safe house or passage."

"Of course not," I said, even though I didn't agree with Harrison's assessment. Carter would never want Ida Belle and Gertie remaining in a dangerous situation. He would be all for them being locked away where no one could get to them and they couldn't get into any trouble. As for me, he'd probably prefer if I just disappeared.

He might get his wish.

If we managed to get Ahmad in New Orleans, there would be no reason for me to stay in Sinful. I could become a ghost as far as Sinful was concerned...just like Max. The only difference was, I would never return.

Chapter Sixteen

I knew I was supposed to wait on Ida Belle's call and for her to pick me up, and given the situation, it wasn't in my best interest to go walking down the streets of Sinful alone after dark, but I honestly didn't care. I'd reached that mental state of "what happens is going to happen" and there was no shaking me out of that attitude until I was ready to listen to logic again.

Besides, I was going stir-crazy in that silent house. Turning on the television hadn't provided one ounce of distraction, and Merlin, while a decent enough housemate, wasn't exactly a conversationalist. He'd watched the entire night unfold from his latest preferred position at the top of the stairs. I decided that if reincarnation was real, I wanted to come back as a cat. Aside from being startled during sleep, very little perturbed them.

I checked the street from my bedroom window and pulled on a ball cap, shoving my ponytail underneath. The streets were clear—not even so much as a car passing by—but I still let myself out through the back door and skirted through my neighbor's backyard before making my way around to the front of the houses. Front doors were too easily watched from a distance. A couple cars I didn't recognize were parked down the block from me. Most likely, they were friends or relatives of the people who lived in the houses, but why run the risk?

I set out at a good clip for Main Street. For someone with my conditioning, it wasn't a long jog. For someone in my state of mind, it wasn't long enough. When I got close to downtown, I turned and set off down another block, increasing my pace to a sprint. I'd circled the block twice and was dripping with sweat before I stopped and bent over, drawing in big gulps of air. After a couple minutes' recovery, I checked my cell phone but still hadn't received a message from Ida Belle.

I looked at my watch. It had been forty-five minutes since they'd left my house. They had to be close to wrapping things up. I'd just head over there now and wait until they finished. I could use some water, and I wasn't going back home for it. I set off at my jogging pace again and a couple minutes later stepped inside the sheriff's department.

Deputy Breaux looked up from the front desk when I entered. His eyes widened as he took in my somewhat disheveled appearance. "Are you all right?" he asked as he jumped up from his desk.

"I'm fine. I just jogged over."

Deputy Breaux frowned. "I don't think it's a good idea to be jogging around by yourself, especially at night. I'll go right ahead and admit this thing with those men at Gertie's house has scared the crap out of me."

"It's certainly upsetting," I said. "My problem is I've always exercised when I'm stressed, and Marge didn't have a treadmill. I was going stir-crazy just sitting there listening to the silence."

Deputy Breaux relaxed a little. "I can see that. When I'm really stressed, I fish, but my sister gets on one of those step machines. She's been through two of them already in the last five years. You gotta wonder what she's doing to her knees."

And what was stressing her out enough to wear out two stair-climbers. As far as I knew, Deputy Breaux's sister was a stay-at-home mom with two elementary-aged children. Don't get me wrong—that setup would probably drive me to drink, but it was the life she wanted. "Maybe you should see about getting her checked out by a doctor," I said. I'd seen plenty of agents crack and need anxiety meds to function normally. "She might have something wrong with her that exercise can't fix."

Deputy Breaux nodded. "Mom says she's been different ever since she fell at the boat dock. She cracked her head good. I think Mom finally got her to agree to see a doctor in New Orleans."

"Good. I hope that helps."

"Thank you." He gave me a shy smile. "You're a really nice person, Ms. Morrow, always thinking about other people."

I just smiled. What was the alternative? Tell him I wasn't a nice person at all? That most everything I did was self-serving even if it appeared altruistic?

The desk phone rang and Deputy Breaux answered.

"Yep. That's good," he said. "I'll be there in a couple minutes." He hung up the phone and looked at me. "The crime scene unit is done processing Gertie's house. I've got to go secure it. The neighbors have already started collecting on the sidewalk. I don't even know what I'm supposed to say to them."

"That you can't speak about an ongoing investigation and that Gertie is fine and wasn't at home when the incident occurred."

He relaxed a little. "That sounds good. I'm going to say it just like you told me. Will you be all right staying up here alone? You can lock the door after I leave."

"I'll be fine."

"Okay then. They're back in Carter's office doing the statements. I'm sure you won't be waiting long."

"No problem, and Deputy Breaux, be careful."

"Yes, ma'am."

I waited until he got into his truck, then locked the front

door behind him. Under normal circumstances, I would have headed straight behind the desk and started flipping through all the paperwork, but I couldn't work up the energy to care. What I really needed was water, so I headed down the hall for the break room.

The makeshift "Broken" sign on the bathroom door almost made me smile, until I remembered that Carter probably considered it just one more time he'd been made a fool of. He'd probably spent every free moment over the past couple of hours putting the past five weeks into perspective. He wasn't going to like what he remembered. Not cast in a new light.

The break room was down the hallway at the back of the building. The door to Carter's office was closed and I could hear muffled voices inside. I stepped into the break room and pulled a bottled water from the refrigerator. I was about to head back up front when the air-conditioning turned off and Gertie's voice flooded through the air vent as clear as day.

"You can't just pass judgment on her without knowing the facts," Gertie said.

I froze.

"Says the only two people who knew the truth?" Carter asked. "You'll understand if I don't really care much for you mounting a defense."

"She didn't tell us," Ida Belle said. "We knew."

"Yeah, that's what she said, and I don't buy it for a minute. What I saw tonight was Krav Maga, executed with the precision of a highly trained assassin. Soldiers weren't using that art in Vietnam, and whatever they used back then, they certainly weren't running through the hospitals and offices doing it."

"We saw it in the field," Ida Belle said. "We weren't administrative staff. Gertie, Marge, and I were counterintelligence."

There was a long pause of silence, then finally Carter said, "You expect me to believe that?"

"Yes. I do," Ida Belle said. "Our military records are sealed, of course, but I'm still in contact with our commanding officer. I'm sure he'd be happy to fill you in on the finer points of our training and experience. Do you really think two average old ladies would take the risks we do?"

"I...I don't know what to think anymore. Jesus."

"We're really sorry to lay it on you like this," Gertie said. "No one in Sinful has ever known our past and that's the way we wanted it. Marge, Ida Belle, and I made a pact to never talk about it."

"And we kept it," Ida Belle said, "until we met Fortune. We couldn't pretend we didn't know what she was and we knew she wouldn't trust us unless she knew what we were. What we knew for certain is that she was in danger and we wanted to help her."

"Exactly," Gertie said. "So if you have a problem with Fortune lying, even though it was a federal offense for her to tell you the truth, then you have to be just as angry with us. After all, we've been lying to you your entire life."

"Your lies don't have the same impact," Carter said.

"We know that," Gertie said, "and we're not trying to diminish what you're going through. We're just trying to explain why it was necessary."

"Do you think I don't know that?" Carter asked, his voice growing louder. "I served in Iraq. Do you have any idea what I did there?"

"No," Ida Belle said.

"That's because you're not supposed to," Carter said. "Just like I don't hand over facts on open investigations because you ask for them or allow you to get involved in police matters because you want to. I understand professional responsibility and am a big fan. But that doesn't excuse personal involvement."

"So she should have kept telling you no," Gertie said, "regardless of how persistent you were or how attracted she was? I see. That's a pretty wide brush of judgment you're swinging there. Maybe if you knew the things we did, you'd feel differently about the choices she made."

"If I knew the things you did," he said, "this entire discussion would have never been necessary. Now, if you don't mind, I'd like to get this next part over with. I appreciate what the two of you are trying to do. I know your heart is in the right place. And don't worry about my repeating anything you told me. Your secret will remain one, at least as far as I'm concerned."

I hurried out of the break room and back to the front. I pulled out a chair at an empty desk and sat down, then pulled out my phone and started a game. At the last minute, I realized the bottled water would give me away and I managed to get it into the trash can before the three of them walked out from the hallway.

They drew up short when they saw me sitting there.

"How did you get here?" Ida Belle asked.

"I jogged."

"You shouldn't have left the house alone," Gertie said. "It's not safe."

"Yeah, that's what people keep telling me. I think it's a little too late for everyone to worry about my safety. Being in danger is part of my job description." I rose from my chair. "Are you ready to take my statement?"

Carter had been frowning the entire time, looking over my shoulder and not directly at me. "I've already typed one up," he said, finally locking his eyes on mine. "I just need a signature on that pack of lies so that neither of us has to go into uncomfortable details."

So that's how it was going to be. He was making sure he didn't have to spend any more time alone with me than absolutely necessary. Well, no need to inconvenience him for even a minute. "Great." I looked at Ida Belle and Gertie. "I need you two to come as well. I have instructions from my partner and they involve you."

They nodded and everyone headed back to Carter's office. I dragged an extra chair in from the break room, closed the door, and took a seat. Carter pushed a piece of paper across the table to me and I read my "statement" as written by Carter. It was basically the same lie he'd told Deputy Breaux, with enough detail to make it sound real but not so much as to raise eyebrows.

"Will that work for your people?" Carter asked when I finished reading.

"As long as it keeps me from being arrested, my people will be happy." I grabbed a pen and signed the document, breaking two more laws when I did. One, it was all lies. Two, I wasn't Sandy-Sue Morrow. But as long as it didn't draw any unwanted attention to me, I didn't care. At the moment, there were a lot of things I didn't care about.

I pushed the document back to Carter and he put it in a file. After a couple seconds of uncomfortable silence, I turned to Ida Belle and Gertie. "I talked to Harrison. They're pulling us from Sinful and placing us in a safe house in New Orleans."

"What about the leak?" Ida Belle asked.

"Harrison and Director Morrow are the only people at the CIA who will know the location of the safe house and who is staying there," I said.

"How will we get there?" Gertie asked.

"Harrison is arranging transport," I said. "My guess is it will not be a limo. Expect unconventional. We can't afford to be followed."

They both nodded and I looked over at Carter. "I assume you don't have an issue with any of this?"

He cocked his head to one side. "Would it matter if I did?"

"No."

"Then why ask? But to answer your question, I'm happy to have the problem moved out of Sinful. I'm not thrilled that Sinful residents are caught up in the middle of it, but then, unlike the rest of us, they knew what the risks were when they jumped in with both feet."

I struggled not to wince at his barb. He really wasn't taking this well. Gertie shook her head and frowned. Ida Belle gave him a disapproving look.

"If you want to act like an injured child," Ida Belle said, "you're welcome to, of course. But it's not going to get you anywhere with the three of us. What's happening right now is more important than your personal life, and while you may think the problem is leaving when Fortune exits Sinful, you're wrong. The counterfeiter has a contact here and that person is yet undiscovered. You can sit around and pretend everything is great or you can get over yourself and do the job I know you're capable of doing. The woman you *claimed* to care about is in a life-and-death situation. You can either be part of the solution or part of the problem."

Carter flushed, and I could tell Ida Belle's words had not only pissed him off but embarrassed him. I wasn't certain it was the best line of attack to take, but it seemed to be the most efficient.

"You're right," he said. "I will devote my time to finding the contact, assuming the federal government is going to allow me to do my job."

"There are no requests from the CIA," I said, "other than to try to maintain my cover. The agency is happy for any help you can provide. But you can't let on that you're looking for a counterfeiter or it will get back to the men we're tracking. Then they'll know you have a federal contact and will be expecting a setup."

Carter nodded. "I'll go about my normal work but I'll keep my eyes on Brody Sampson. If he's the Sinful connection, those four dead men should make him flinch."

"What about Ally?" Gertie asked. "She can't stay at your house."

"No, she can't," I agreed. "What is the official story you plan on releasing about what happened at Gertie's house?" I asked Carter.

"That four men were in the process of burglarizing the home. The men had apparently gotten into an argument among themselves and two were killed before I arrived to check the house because of the alarm. The remaining two men rushed me in the backyard and I dispatched them."

"Good," I said. "The less information, the better, and treating all four of them as part of the same crew makes it easier to keep things straight. I'll work up a cover story for Ally that will get her out of my house and explain why the three of us are leaving town."

"Where will she go?" Gertie said. "Her house isn't secure yet."

"She can stay with my mother," Carter said. "Just let me know what you tell Ally so I can use the same story as well."

"Thanks," I said. I felt a ton better knowing Ally would stay with Carter's mother. That meant Carter would have eyes on her even when he couldn't be there. I didn't think Ally was at risk, but I wanted to be extra careful. There were still too many unknowns. If something happened to Ally because of me, I'd never forgive myself.

"And what's the story for you guys leaving town?" Carter asked.

"Girls' trip," I said. "If anyone asks, we're going to Florida. My Jeep will be locked in the garage, so no one will be the wiser."

"Any idea when the transport will happen?" Carter asked.

"As quickly as possible," I said. "My guess is we'll be gone tomorrow."

He nodded. "As soon as you let me know that you've talked to Ally, I'll call my mother." He looked down at the floor a moment, then frowned. "I assume this is the last contact we'll have?"

"Yes," I said. "From any of us. You can send us messages but we probably won't be able to answer. I suspect they'll take our phones." I wrote a number on a piece of paper and handed it to Carter. "That is my partner's direct cell number. His name is Harrison. If you find out anything that he needs to know, call that number."

Carter took the number and stuck it in his wallet. "This takedown that the CIA is hoping to stage. Any idea when it will happen?"

"No. But it will be soon. Once Ahmad and Randal realize their men are dead, things will heat up quickly."

"And what you're really hoping is that this Ahmad will show?"

"Yes."

Carter nodded and was silent for several seconds. "And if you're successful, what does that mean for you?"

What did it mean for me? Good Lord. Where did I start? It meant I didn't have to pretend to be someone else any longer. It meant I had to face the music at the CIA for all my transgressions. It meant I could leave Sinful and go back to everything I knew and was comfortable with in DC. It also meant deciding whether I wanted to return to my old life, if that was even possible.

"It means I get to go back to being Fortune Redding," I said.

Whoever that was.

Chapter Seventeen

It was a somber threesome that made its way into my house. No one had to say a word, but we all trailed back to the kitchen and pulled out the whiskey. We had our first round in silence, everyone mulling over what had happened and what was to come. After Gertie poured the second round, I decided to break the silence.

"I heard what you said to Carter," I said.

They both stared at me, slightly surprised.

"I was getting a bottled water," I explained. "Your voices carried through the air vent into the break room when the AC cut off. You didn't have to tell him. You've kept your past a secret all this time."

"It was something we felt needed to be done," Ida Belle said.

Gertie nodded.

"There was no point," I said. "I heard his reaction as clearly as I heard your confession. You wasted your secret on someone who isn't capable of understanding the point."

"He's not capable right now," Gertie said, "but give him time."

"Normally," Ida Belle said, "I wouldn't give touchy-feely advice, but in this case, I agree with Gertie. Carter has been hit with a rash of crap that has nothing to do with his personal life. His job is at constant risk and more importantly, the town and people he cares about are at risk as well. And he's still not at one hundred percent. I know he wants everyone to think he's fine, but I've had a concussion. You don't return to normal that quickly."

"God, isn't that the truth," Gertie said. "I've had the aftereffects of a concussion last for weeks."

"You've had the aftereffects of a concussion for the last fifty years," Ida Belle said. "Anyway, he's got all of that mess on his plate and isn't firing on all cylinders to begin with, so when your secret came out, it was the whole straw-camel thing."

Gertie nodded. "And I'm not saying this to make you feel worse, but I'd bet he felt the only good thing he had going was his relationship with you."

"Great," I said. "I'm single-handedly responsible for destroying the man's life."

"No," Ida Belle said firmly. "You're not responsible for anything but your deception, and that was an unfortunate requirement of your situation. Everything else that has happened in this town is the result of criminal activity. All of which was already here. It's not like you bagged it up and brought it with you like a plague."

"Maybe not," I said, "but you have to admit, the timing is crappy. I look like the Pied Piper of bad guys…just leading wherever I go."

"It's a shame you can't lead them into the middle of the Antarctic," Gertie said, "then teleport out."

"That would be a neat trick," I agreed, "but the CIA would have to give me a raise. Look, I know you guys are trying to make me feel better, and I don't disagree with anything you're saying. I know Carter is overwhelmed with really, really bad stuff happening in his town, and I know, probably better than anyone, that he's not a hundred percent. He tries not to let it show, but to someone like me, who's trained to lock in on any weakness, I can tell he's not the superhero he usually is."

"Do you think he needs backup?" Gertie asked.

"Not in the general way," I said. "Trust me, he took that shot on Ahmad's guy without hesitation and it was a direct hit between the eyes. He's not a hundred percent but he's close enough to be deadly as hell, because he was far better than the average lawman to begin with. I'm not worried about Carter as long as he goes about town business and doesn't let on that he knows about the counterfeiting."

Ida Belle nodded. "He's smart enough to keep cover, and he knows the stakes."

"It's going to be hard for him," Gertie said, "knowing what's going on beneath his nose and not attacking it the way he normally would. Especially with your life on the line. He's hurt, but he still cares about you. That's not something you can turn on and off."

"Have you thought about what you're going to do," Ida Belle asked, "if this takedown is successful?"

I blew out a breath. "I haven't thought about much else the entire night."

"And?"

"And I'm no closer to an answer now than I was hours ago."

Gertie poured another round of whiskey. "I can't imagine how difficult your situation is. When Ida Belle, Marge, and I finished up our last tour in Vietnam, we knew we were coming home and never leaving American soil again. We had our backstories in place and were doing decent financially and had job prospects already lined up. We knew exactly what kind of life we wanted, even before we went to Vietnam."

Ida Belle nodded. "I think it was our complete

understanding of what we wanted that sent us to Vietnam in the first place—to protect the dream."

I felt a sense of pride swell in me. Not for myself but for these two women. They were everything I wanted to be someday—successful, happy, dedicated to their town and its people, and most importantly they knew who they were.

"Do you miss the work?" Ida Belle asked.

"Yes," I said without hesitation. "My involvement with things here gives that away. I'm not made for a slow, domestic life. I know that much about myself. You two, of all people, should appreciate that."

"That's a start," Ida Belle said. "What is it about the work you miss?"

"I'm not going to lie. I love the thrill of closing in on a mark. I love knowing that the world is a slightly better place because of what I do. And egotistically, I love knowing that only a handful of people are capable of doing my job."

Ida Belle nodded. "Have you ever thought about leaving? Not since you've been in Sinful, but before?"

I frowned. Had I ever considered leaving the CIA? I honestly couldn't remember a time that I had, and then it hit me why that was. "No," I said quietly. "It's the only thing that defined me."

Gertie and Ida Belle looked at each other and the concern I saw in their expressions was both comforting and overwhelming.

"You mentioned before that your father was an agent," Gertie said.

"Not just an agent," I said. "My father was one of the best agents the CIA has ever had."

"Big shoes to fill," Gertie said.

"Impossible shoes to fill," I said.

"But that hasn't stopped you from trying," Gertie said.

"No. I guess it hasn't."

"Were you trying to prove you were good enough to him?" Gertie asked, "or yourself?"

I shook my head. "Jesus. Him? Both? I don't think I know anymore."

"You started down a path," Ida Belle said, "with one destination in mind. I get that. The problem is you never adjusted for changes that happened during your travels."

"I guess it was easier to just keep doing what I already knew."

"Well," Ida Belle said, "you certainly don't have to decide your future sitting at this table tonight, but I think you need to put it at the top of your list. Even if the takedown is successful, you can't ever go back to what you were before. Not entirely."

"I know."

Things had changed. I had changed. I'd fought so hard against coming to Sinful, but it was the best gift I'd ever been given. I'd opened my eyes to the world outside of my job. I'd formed relationships with people based on something other than my work. I'd started to believe that I could matter to people. People who had no preconceived notion of who I should be. Despite all the confidence I had in my ability to do my job, I hadn't had any in myself as a person.

Not until Sinful.

"As part of your considering," Gertie said, "we want you to know that we'd be thrilled if you chose to stay here. We know it wouldn't be easy to explain yourself to everyone, and you'd have to figure out a job and such, but please don't write it off."

Ida Belle nodded. "And if you just need time to consider your options, you can stay with Gertie or me as long as you like."

I felt the tears well up in my eyes again. After my mom's death, I'd spent a lifetime surrounded by people who wanted something from me. These women simply wanted me.

It was beyond overwhelming.

It was a long, hard night. I slept in ten-minute increments, awakened by every creak of the house. Merlin finally tired of my constant shifting and sighing and stalked out of the room for a quieter place to sleep. I had hoped the whiskey would slow down my churning mind, but it didn't seem to make any difference at all. It whirled all night like a carnival ride, constantly shifting from one crisis to another, never lingering long enough to come to a determination on anything.

I finally gave up and climbed out of bed at 5:00 a.m. It was foolish to keep pretending I was going to sleep, especially in this house. It wouldn't take much effort to track Gertie back to me. If Harrison wasn't ready with the safe house today, then I was going to take them out of Sinful myself. We could transfer from wherever I decided we would hole up.

I had just poured my first cup of coffee when I heard the front door open. Ally stepped into the kitchen a minute later, looking a bit surprised.

"You're up early," she said.

"I had trouble sleeping."

She gave me a critical look and poured herself a cup of coffee. "You look like you fought a war," she said as she took a seat across from me. "Is something wrong?"

"Ha. Yeah, you could say that."

"Do you want to talk about it?"

"No, but I don't have a choice as part of what's wrong involves you."

"Me?" Ally's eyes widened. "What did I do?"

"You didn't do anything. I did. Or technically, Ida Belle,

Gertie, and I did."

"Francine got a call last night from one of Gertie's neighbors. He said the police carried four body bags out of Gertie's backyard. I had just texted with you so I knew you guys were watching movies. Francine said the neighbor is an old drunk and we shrugged it off. Are you telling me he wasn't as drunk as we thought he was?"

"He might have been drunk, but he wasn't wrong."

Ally's hand flew up and covered her mouth. "Oh my God. Who were they?"

"We don't know. Carter and I went by there last night because Gertie's alarm was going off. Apparently, it's always been sketchy, so no one thought anything of it. I was going to pick up a chair she requested from her shed while Carter checked the back windows, but then two guys rushed us and Carter took them out. He found two more bodies in the bushes."

"That's unbelievable. No wonder you didn't sleep. You must have been scared to death."

"I'm okay. I mean, it's not something I ever want to see again, but that's not the worst part. I can't give you the details because I would be breaking the law if I did, but the bottom line is that Ida Belle, Gertie, and I stumbled into something when we went to New Orleans. Something we weren't supposed to see."

All of the color fled Ally's face. "You think they were there to kill you?"

"Yeah. So until the police can figure out what's going on, the three of us are going to be relocated to a safe house, and you can't stay here. It isn't safe. Carter is going to arrange for you to stay with his mother."

"Oh my God, Fortune. It's like a bad movie. Of course you have to hide, and I'll be fine with Emmaline. Are you sure she'll be safe with me staying there?"

I nodded. "They're not looking for you. But they have Gertie's license plate and they saw me. It wouldn't take much to track her back to me. I don't want you caught in the cross fire."

"There's not going to be any," Ally said. "All that's going to be left here is an empty house and thank goodness for that. Can you tell me where you're going?"

"No. We probably won't know until we get there. And I won't be able to contact you until it's over. If you need to tell me something, leave me a message or send a text. If they don't take my phone, I'll read them, but that's all I can do. If you have an emergency, get in touch with Carter. For his own protection, he won't know where we are either, but he'll have a way to reach someone who will."

Ally shook her head. "I just can't believe it. So many odd things have happened in Sinful lately, but this is the worst. Promise me the three of you will sit in that safe house, surrounded by guards, and not move even a step until the police have this all fixed. No taking chances."

"I promise."

She narrowed her eyes at me. "Hold out your hands."

I smiled. She knew me entirely too well. I held my hands up, spreading my fingers apart. She nodded, then looked under the table at my legs.

"Okay," she said, seeming satisfied. "I believe you…this time."

It was a safe bet. The Feds were going to lock the three of us up like prisoners. We probably wouldn't even get to pee without an escort…not if the bathroom contained a window. All the windows would be covered and the blinds and shades drawn. No food delivery. No flow of people in and out. It would be stocked with a minimum of a week's food and toiletry supply for us and however many guards would be placed with us. My guess is only two or three simply because Harrison could only trust so many people given the CIA leak. But it would be too many people to circumvent. Even if we wanted to.

"I don't know when we'll be leaving," I said, "but my guess is it will be today. I think it's a good idea for you to go ahead and pack and relocate this morning. I'll call Carter and let him know when you're ready. I'm really sorry about this."

Ally shook her head. "Don't you dare apologize. I know you guys are usually into things better left alone, but your hearts are in the right place. And the truth is, you've helped get some bad people out of Sinful."

She rose from the table, still clutching her coffee. "I best head upstairs and pack a bag. What am I supposed to tell people when they ask?"

"Tell them we're taking a girls' trip to Florida."

"I wish that was the truth."

"Me too."

###

At 3:00 p.m., after a silent ride with Carter to the hospital, we stood in the morgue alongside FBI Agent Moss, looking at our mode of escape.

"No way," Gertie said. "I'll just stay in Sinful and let them kill me."

"Either way," Ida Belle said, "you'll wind up in one of these." She waved a hand at the three coffins in front of us.

"I won't know about it then," Gertie said. "Don't tell me this doesn't creep you out."

"It's got a morbid vibe to it," I said, "but it's bulletproof as an escape. Someone could have easily followed us to the hospital, but they would never think to follow coffins out."

Gertie shook her head. "I'll suffocate. Besides, I have claustrophobia."

"You don't have claustrophobia," Ida Belle said. "You're just afraid of death and this is too close for comfort."

"And these coffins have been modified with breathing holes," I said. "See?" I pointed to a panel that looked like wood but was actually a vent.

Gertie leaned forward to inspect it. "How did you know that was there? You've done this before, haven't you? You've traipsed around in a coffin. Good God woman, is there no limit to the things you'll do?"

I stared. "Are you kidding me with that question?"

"Ladies," Agent Moss said. "We need to get a move on. The funeral home has a limited open window for us to unload before people start arriving for a ceremony."

"And you're sure about the funeral home people?" I asked. I knew he had to be or we wouldn't be doing the transfer there, but I couldn't help asking, especially with death being one of Randal's business ventures.

Agent Moss nodded. "Only the funeral director knows what we're doing, and his daughter is an FBI agent."

"Awesome." We couldn't ask for a better setup than that. "Go ahead," I urged Gertie. "You can choose first. I know you like yellow. Look at this lovely gold silk. Doesn't that feel nice?"

"It would feel nice as a nightie, not a wrap of death." Gertie sighed and stared at the coffin.

"It's just for a couple minutes," Agent Moss assured her. "Once we get you into the van, we'll open them up. We'll close them again for a couple minutes to get you inside the funeral home, then it's all over."

"A couple of minutes—here and there?" Gertie said. "You promise that's all?"

He held up three fingers. "Scout's honor."

"I'm not crossing my arms or anything weird," Gertie said.

Ida Belle shook her head and climbed inside one of the coffins. "Close me up," she said. "This may be the only peace I get for the next couple days."

I grinned and shut the lid to the coffin. "How's the air?"

"Great," Ida Belle said. "I could do yoga in here there's so much air."

"Fine," Gertie said and stepped up into the coffin. She closed her eyes after lying down and I saw her lips move as I fastened the lid. I assumed she was praying.

"How are you doing?" I asked.

"Hurry up and get me the hell out of here," she said.

I looked over at Agent Moss. "You got my clothes?" I asked quietly.

He nodded and handed me a black jacket and cap that matched what he was wearing. I replaced my yoga pants with black slacks, pulled the suit jacket over my black T-shirt, stuffed my hair up into the cap, and gave him a thumbs-up. He motioned two more identically dressed agents, who'd been standing guard in the hallway, into the room.

Two of us took each coffin and started rolling them down the hall. We slid both coffins into the back of a black van with the funeral home logo on it, then two of the agents jumped into a black sedan that held the funeral home logo, and the lead agent and I climbed into the van. As soon as we pulled out of the parking lot, I headed to the back of the van and opened the coffins.

Gertie popped up, gasping for air, then locked in on my outfit. "What the hell? Why aren't you in a coffin?"

"Because we could only fit two in the van," I said.

"So? You could have played dead and I could have been the funeral home assistant."

"Sure," I said. "I mean, you would have only had to lift this coffin, which weighs about two hundred fifty pounds plus your body weight, but I'm sure that would have been no problem."

"You'd be surprised what adrenaline can do," Gertie said.

"Stop your bitching," Ida Belle said. "It wasn't that long and I could breathe in there as well as I can in my own bed. The silk is nice. I might have to get some sheets like that."

"How do we look?" I asked Agent Moss.

He picked up a radio and contacted the other agents, asking for a report.

Clear.

That single word relayed back a couple seconds later and I felt some of the tension in my shoulders release. No one had followed us.

"So we're good?" Gertie asked.

"For the moment," I said. "We've still got to get to the safe house, but no one is following us."

"Great," Gertie said. "I don't suppose we could stop at an IHOP or something. I'm starving."

"I think you're going to have to wait," I said.

"The safe house is stocked with food," Agent Moss said. "You should be in place in an hour or so."

Gertie wrestled her purse out from under the lower part of the coffin. I knew I should have insisted the FBI search that purse of doom before they got into the coffins, but selfishly, I knew I might get into a situation where I would welcome something from Gertie's bag of tricks.

"It's a good thing I don't depend on other people," Gertie said. She pulled out a bottle of soda and a package of peanut butter crackers. "I have three of these. Anyone interested?"

"Not unless you're sharing your soda," Ida Belle said. "Those things stick to the roof of my mouth."

Gertie reached into her purse and pulled out two more

sodas.

"What else do you have in there?" I asked.

"None of your business," Gertie said, "but I still contend I could have lifted the coffin."

She was probably right. Gertie's right shoulder had a slight dip and she leaned a bit to the right all the time, I'm sure from the weight of that purse. I wouldn't have been completely surprised if she had rolled a tank out of that bag, just like in the cartoons. I had a bit of concern about what kind of weaponry she was packing—and I'm sure it was extensive—but I couldn't ask about it in front of Agent Moss or he'd confiscate it. I could only pray that the safety was engaged on everything. I grabbed a soda and a package of crackers and took a seat on Ida Belle's coffin.

The ride to the funeral home went quicker than I expected, especially given the lack of conversation during the ride. I knew why I was silent. I had more to think about than any twenty people usually did in an entire lifetime. I wasn't sure what Ida Belle and Gertie were dwelling on, but their occasional glances at me and then each other made me think it was probably the same things I was dwelling on.

Agent Moss had been short on words since we'd met, but that was standard operating procedure for Feds. Per Morrow's direction, the FBI wasn't to know my true identity, so Agent Moss wouldn't see any reason to speak to me as an associate. We were just three women who'd witnessed something we shouldn't have seen and needed to be secured.

The only thing I refused to allow myself to think about was Carter. Every time my thoughts attempted to shift to him, I forced a change of direction. My doomed relationship wasn't a factor in my decisions. I needed to make a logical, responsible decision about my future. Thoughts of Carter and what might have been had no place in my consideration.

Unfortunately, I didn't know how the takedown would go or how my reception at the CIA would be afterward, and both were huge factors in my decision-making. Or maybe they weren't. Maybe if Director Morrow told me I could return to the CIA but had to answer the phones for a year, I'd apologize and go back to DC like a good little soldier. If only Gertie had a crystal ball in that bag of hers. Life had been so much easier when I only had one thing to do and someone else usually made decisions for me.

As we pulled up to the back entrance at the funeral home, I closed Ida Belle and Gertie back up and took my seat next to Agent Moss. He parked and we headed to the back of the van to unload. The two agents following us arrived a minute later. The funeral home director poked his head out the rear door and motioned to us to collect the transport carts in the hallway behind him.

"You've got about thirty minutes before people start arriving for this evening's viewing," he said. He glanced at the coffins. "Are you sure they're okay in there?"

"Of course we're not okay," Gertie yelled. "We're alive and in coffins."

The funeral director blanched and his hands shook as he pushed a transfer cart out the door. Apparently dead people in coffins he could handle, but shove a live one in there, and it freaked him out. It took all kinds.

Agent Moss and I slid Ida Belle's coffin onto the cart and pushed it to the side while the other two agents pulled Gertie's coffin onto the cart.

And that's where our great plan blew up right in our faces.

Chapter Eighteen

I saw the cart move forward as the agents made their final pull on the coffin to get it completely on the cart, but by the time I yelled and leaped for the cart, it was already rolling away.

"Idiots!" Agent Moss yelled as we took off running.

I ran like an Olympic sprinter, but the odds were against me. The parking lot sloped down and the weight of the coffin made it gain speed in a way I couldn't manage. I prayed it veered to the left and hit the curb. It wouldn't be the most comfortable way to unload, but it beat the alternative. Unfortunately, the alternative was the cart's selection, and it shot out of the driveway and down the alley. I could hear Gertie screaming as it bumped along.

I didn't think it was possible, but I dialed up my speed another notch. Agent Moss couldn't keep pace, but I could hear his footsteps pounding close behind me. The entire time I ran, I watched the busy street at the end of the alley and prayed the cart would veer left or right. If it shot into traffic, that would be very bad. The last thing I wanted was for Gertie to actually die in that coffin. That would be an irony that didn't have a bit of humor connected to it.

The coffin was about twenty yards from the end of the alley when I closed in on it, only five feet away. It had just cleared a section of fencing and was about to skirt a back driveway when a hot dog vendor pushed his cart into the alley. The coffin hit the vendor cart right in the side, tipping the entire thing over and scattering wieners and buns all over the alley. The vendor, who was knocked down by the initial impact, jumped up, ready to raise hell over his cart, then took one look at the coffin tipped on its side and paled.

As I rushed up to the side of the coffin, the top flew open and Gertie started crawling out. The hot dog vendor made the sign of the cross, then passed out right in the middle of a stack of buns. I reached down to help Gertie up as she struggled to get to her feet. Agent Moss ran up beside me, surveying the damage and looking like he was about to have a heart attack.

"Get her out of here," he said. "I'll fix this."

"Wait," Gertie said and reached back inside the coffin for her purse.

"Hurry up," I said.

She took two steps, then stopped. "Are those beef?" She bent over and started picking up wieners and buns, stuffing them into her purse.

I grabbed her arm and pulled. "You have to get out of sight."

Gertie slung the purse over her shoulder and we ran back up the alley and into the funeral home. We dashed into the room secured for unloading and collapsed on two chairs. Ida Belle hurried over as soon as we entered.

"Are you all right?" she asked. "I heard screaming and the funeral director looks like he's going to cry, but no one will tell me what happened."

"Considering I almost died in that coffin," Gertie said, "I'm doing okay. But I'm going to feel it tomorrow." She pulled a wiener and bun out of her purse and put them together. "Anyone else want one? I have quite a few."

Ida Belle looked over at me, her confusion apparent.

"Later," I said as the funeral home director ran into the room, muttering and wiping his sweating, bald forehead with a silk handkerchief. Ida Belle was right. He did look ready to cry.

"This is a tragedy," he said. "How can I possibly explain this? My reputation will be ruined."

"Agent Moss is going to handle it," I said. "Stop worrying."

The funeral director looked a tiny bit hopeful but not convinced. I couldn't really blame him. Agent Moss could throw money at the vendor for the cart repairs and the loss of revenue and stock, but it would require an exorcism to make him unsee Gertie crawling out of that coffin.

"Is the SUV out front?" I asked the other two agents, who'd left Agent Moss to deal with everything and would probably be hearing about it for the next month or two.

One of them nodded.

"Then go get it and bring it around back," I said. "And don't screw up this time."

They started to hesitate. After all, to them I was just some broad who needed protection, but apparently their embarrassment at allowing Gertie to get away overrode any indignation of being ordered around by a civilian, because they filed silently out of the room.

Agent Moss entered a couple minutes later. "Everything's settled with the vendor," he assured the funeral director. "I told him we were a private transport company and not affiliated with your funeral home. He has a contact number to call with a damage amount and we'll be issuing him a check."

"Thank God." The funeral director slid into a chair, his entire body seeming to relax into jelly. I hoped he could work up the energy to run his viewing. It would start any minute.

"I sent the agents to get the SUV," I said.

Agent Moss nodded. "They were pulling around when I

came in the back door. I've already removed the decals from the car and van. I'll call for someone to pick up them up as soon as we leave. We need to get out of here now before people start arriving."

We headed out of the funeral home and into the SUV. The door had barely closed behind us when I heard the lock slide into place. I'd never seen a man happier to get rid of people than the funeral home director had been.

I climbed into the second row of seats next to one of the other agents and looked out the limo-tinted windows as we drove. I didn't know New Orleans very well, but I had no doubt Ida Belle and Gertie were watching and would know where the safe house was located within the city. I knew it didn't matter as we were supposed to stay put, but something about not knowing my exact location bothered me. Navigating the bayous around Sinful with Ida Belle and Gertie had always frustrated me. If I didn't know any better, I would swear some of them shifted overnight.

We were still somewhere near downtown when Agent Moss turned onto a side street and parked at the curb in front of an old two-story brick building. The red brick was chipped and crumbling, but no more so than any of the other historical buildings surrounding it. We exited the SUV and Agent Moss waved us inside and upstairs. At the top of the stairs was a single locked door. Agent Moss unlocked the door and we followed him inside.

It was a studio apartment and wasn't a big space—maybe eight hundred square feet total—but it had been equipped for our stay. Three twin beds lined one wall where big venetian screen room dividers stood next to them. I assumed that was our sleeping quarters. Agents Two and Three were on guard duty and I supposed would share the couch on their off shift. Agent Moss had other things to oversee and looked more than ready to ditch all of us.

The kitchen was small but serviceable, and the pantry and refrigerator were well stocked. I was a bit concerned about five people and one tiny bathroom, but it wasn't exactly something that could be fixed. I pulled off my cap and the suit and tossed them onto one of the beds.

"I guess this is home," I said.

Gertie sat her purse on the middle bed and flopped down beside it. "Those hot dogs gave me heartburn. I don't suppose there's an Alka-Seltzer in that pantry, is there?"

Ida Belle opened the pantry door and peered inside. "Doesn't look like it."

"There's a drugstore around the corner," Agent Two said. "Make a list of anything that you need and I'll go pick it up."

We poked around in the kitchen and the bathroom, put together a short list of necessities, and Agent Two headed out. Agent Three flopped down on the couch and a couple minutes later, was snoring.

I took advantage of that opportunity to pick the lock on the drawer Agent Two had locked our cell phones in and handed them out. "Put them on vibrate and no making calls. If they see us with these, they'll break them next time."

"Some security they are," Gertie said as she stuffed the phone in her pocket. "The first one goes shopping and the second one takes a nap." She reached inside her purse and pulled out a .45. It's a good thing I have my own backup."

"Put that away," I said. "If they see it, they'll confiscate it. Why do you think mine's hidden in my bra?"

We looked over at Ida Belle, wondering where her pistol was secured.

"I'll never tell," she said.

"Where are we, anyway?" I asked.

"The Warehouse District," Ida Belle said. "But I'm not sure exactly where. I don't know this area that well. I made a note of the street names, though."

"I think we're on the edge of it," Gertie said. She went to the front window and pulled the blinds up a bit. "Hey, isn't that the group home that Landon was in?"

Ida Belle and I peered out the blinds at the large building across the street. It looked like an old school or government building. A weathered sign on the front of it read Haven Place.

"Yeah," Ida Belle said. "That was it."

I watched as a woman in scrubs helped a man out of a car and up the sidewalk to the entry of the building. "I thought you said it closed."

Gertie nodded. "That's what Nora told me."

Ida Belle snorted. "Nora's been drunk for the last fifteen years. This spring she marched into the sheriff's department and claimed her cows had been abducted by aliens."

"Sounds perfectly reasonable for Sinful," I said.

"She doesn't have any cows," Ida Belle said.

"That does not negate my previous statement," I said.

"Well," Gertie said, "if that's the place then we're definitely in the Warehouse District. This is the south side of it."

"How close are we to the art gallery?" I asked.

"Not close," Gertie said. "I mean, not as far as the Warehouse District goes. We're on the other side from the art gallery. Maybe eight blocks?"

I hadn't seen anything to indicate that the gallery was where the money was being printed, but I figured Max would have picked something nearby. But then, I could be completely off. Maybe he was so dedicated to his belief that he was an artist that's why he picked that apartment, and the printing facility was in Mississippi or Idaho. At this point, who knew?

"So what do we do now?" Gertie asked.

I headed to the kitchen bar and pulled three beers out of the refrigerator. "We wait."

That was always the hardest part.

***

I had fallen asleep sitting at the bar when my cell phone buzzed that night around 10:00 p.m. Agent Two was snoring away on the couch, but Agent Three hurried over to hover. "Where did you get that?" he asked, pointing at the phone.

I ignored him. "It's the CIA guy," I said, trying to sound like a civilian.

"Hello," I answered.

"It's Harrison. Is the FBI standing over you?"

"Yes. We're fine. Thanks."

"I'll take that as a yes, so just listen. There's been a change in plans. Using the Randal connection, we've located the printing shop. We fed the information to Ahmad's men in New Orleans."

"So there's more?" I had figured that was the case. Ahmad usually sent backup for backup.

"Yeah. The two dispatched in Sinful weren't the ones our guys were on in New Orleans. There's four in New Orleans that we know of, maybe more. You know Ahmad."

"Oh yeah. What about that one?" Harrison would know I meant Ahmad himself.

"He was spotted two blocks away in a coffee shop, but he slipped out with a group of tourists. We don't have eyes on him now."

I forced my expression to remain neutral but my pulse shot through the roof. I could hear my heart pounding in my ears, and the entire room seemed to expand out, then in. This was it. The

JANA DELEON

moment I'd been praying for over the last two months. Ahmad was within my reach.

"Anyway," Harrison said, "the four just left their hotel and are headed in the direction of the printing shop. Randal arrived ten minutes ago with some of his men, and they did not look like art critics."

"And you're just now telling me this?" What the hell was wrong with him? The whole thing might be over before I got there.

"What's wrong?" Three asked.

I waved a hand at him.

"The print shop is only two blocks from you," Harrison said. "Hand the phone to the agent and I'll tell him to get you outside because we need you to point out the men."

"Okay."

"Then get your ass outside and prepare for the showdown we've all been waiting for."

"He wants to talk to you," I said and handed my phone to Three.

He frowned and took the call.

"Yeah. Are you sure...no, of course you are. We're on our way now." He disconnected the call and handed me the phone. "He explained what's going to happen?"

"What's wrong?" Ida Belle asked.

"Nothing," I said, "they think they have found those guys. They need me to make sure."

"They don't need us too?" Gertie asked.

I shook my head. "He said one of us would do."

Gertie and Ida Belle looked at each other, their expressions grim.

"Be careful," Ida Belle said.

"Extra careful," Gertie said.

"You know me," I said and gave them a smile. "Careful is my middle name." I winked at them and headed for the door, Three walking practically on top of me. At the doorway, I glanced back and they both gave me a thumbs-up.

This was it. Time to fix my life.

Chapter Nineteen

The driver remained silent the entire drive and dropped me off in a parking garage two blocks away. Harrison exited a stairwell and motioned me over. "It's good to see you, Redding," he said and stuck out his fist.

I bumped his knuckles with mine and smiled. "You too." And I meant it. Harrison and I went head-to-head on some things, but when it came to the work, we trusted each other completely. He was a good guy and a great agent, and there simply weren't that many of them out there.

He led me over to the edge of the parking garage and pointed to a warehouse across the street. "That's our target."

"It's a publishing company," I said, surprised. "Either they're lazy or someone likes irony."

"I don't think they're smart enough for irony. I'm going with easier to explain expensive printing equipment orders. The first and second floors contain the legit portion of the business, but the third floor is an attic, and that's where the tax-exempt portion of things are handled. And you'll never guess who owns the publishing company."

"Randal?"

Harrison nodded. "It took some digging, but after you tipped us off to him we got every agent we could pull on researching business records and finally connected the dots. We did a broad sweep to narrow down the real estate that could house a printing operation, then sent men in as city inspectors, gas meter readers...anything that wouldn't arouse suspicion."

"Smart."

"The dead giveaway stuff was out of sight when our fake building inspector went through the third floor of the publishing company, but he recognized enough of the tools and equipment to know what was really going on up there and why it had been separated from the other production areas."

"Is anyone on site now?"

Harrison nodded. "Randal and two of his men went in about twenty minutes ago."

"So what's the play?"

"I have one of our guys on the inside now. He's got the alarm disabled on the back door, so Ahmad's men can get in clean, and he's got a back window ready for us. As soon as Ahmad's men enter, we'll access the building through that window and follow them upstairs. The FBI has four men on the roof of the building next door. When we enter, they'll cross over to the publishing company roof. On my signal, they'll drop through the skylight. It's on the opposite end of the attic from the printing equipment, so they should have a small window of time to gain cover."

"I take it you're not expecting them to surrender."

"Ha. Are you?"

"Not a chance. Ahmad's man was going to kill me in Gertie's backyard and I looked like Suzy Homemaker. No way those guys are stepping down. So three men including Randal and probably another two to four for Ahmad."

"One more with Ahmad."

"You don't know how hard I'm hoping for that one more." With the FBI support and Harrison and me and our guy on the inside, that made it seven against a potential eight. Eight men heavily into arms dealing who would be equipped with the very best money could buy. But they didn't know we were coming, and that made all the difference in the world.

Harrison pulled a smoke grenade from his pocket and handed it to me. "Do you have a pistol?"

I pulled a nine-millimeter—one of Marge's stock—out of my bra. "I have two more magazines where that came from."

He grinned. "I thought you looked like you'd acquired cleavage since you left."

He motioned me to the corner, reached behind a pole, and pulled out a bulletproof vest. I shrugged off my T-shirt, lifted the extra magazines out of my sports bra, and pulled the vest on. It was never a good idea to wear the vest on the outside of your clothes. In my line of work, that just told the bad guys to shift to head shots.

I pulled my T-shirt back on, secured my pistol and the grenade on my jeans, and slipped the magazines into my pocket.

"Ready?"

"Definitely."

He handed me an assault rifle, and we headed down the stairs and out the back of the building. We skirted down the alley, then a block over and back up the alley of the publishing company. There were no lights on behind the building, and as my feet crunched on glass shards, I knew Harrison had eliminated them earlier today. The moon provided enough light to slip down the alley without tripping over anything and soon, we were crouched behind a Dumpster, across the alley from the window we would use to gain entry.

Harrison touched his headset, indicating he was receiving a message, then he pointed toward the street, held up four fingers, then one.

Ahmad's men were one minute out.

I nodded and we both maintained position, watching for movement. About forty-five seconds later, four men slunk down the alley and jimmied the back door. Harrison and I watched carefully, but no one else entered the alley. Ahmad's men didn't hesitate in the doorway and closed it behind them.

I felt my heart sink. He wasn't coming.

If Ahmad didn't show, then this takedown was great for the FBI but didn't solve any of my problems. Harrison looked over at me and I could tell he was as disappointed as I was. He pulled two black ski masks from his vest and handed me one. I pulled the mask on and started to stand when Harrison grabbed my arm and pointed down the alley. I squinted into the darkness, but everything appeared still. Then I saw it. The tiniest shift of shadow about fifty feet away.

I held my breath as a man walked out from the shadows and toward the back door. His face was turned away from us, but there was no mistaking that walk. It was Ahmad. I looked at Harrison and nodded. Harrison gave me a thumbs-up. I could see the excitement flash in his eyes.

My fingers literally ached as they hovered near the trigger of the assault rifle. It would be so easy to take him out right now. One simple shot and my nightmare would be over. But I couldn't do it. That one shot would blow the entire takedown and put the FBI agents and our man on the inside at terrible risk.

We watched as Ahmad let himself in the back door, then waited. Several seconds later, Harrison touched his headset again and pointed two fingers at me and the back door. As we'd choreographed, Harrison and I rose from our positions, looked around opposite ends of the Dumpster, then moved silently for the window, rifles in ready position.

Harrison eased the window up and peered inside, then

motioned for me to enter. I handed him my rifle, pulled myself over the window ledge, and rolled into the room without a sound. I reached back to get my rifle and Harrison's from him and a couple seconds later, we were both in ready position.

And then my cell phone vibrated.

The only people who had my number were people who wouldn't contact me unless it was important. I tapped Harrison on the shoulder and held up one finger, then pulled out my phone. It was from Carter.

Brody left Sinful. I've followed him to NOLA. He just exited Magazine from 90.

I showed Harrison the message and he nodded and tapped my phone, indicating I should give Carter information on the takedown so that he didn't walk into the middle of cross fire.

In position at Deep South Publishing. All parties are in building and our men are ready to execute takedown. Proceed with extreme caution.

I sent the message and a second later the reply came.

10-4.

I nodded to Harrison and he peered out the door, then moved into the hallway. We headed down the hallway and skirted the edges of the reception area to get to the back stairwell. At the base of the stairwell was our inside agent. He pointed up, then held up three fingers.

Everyone was on the third floor, the attic.

Harrison took point and indicated for me to take the rear position, and we headed up the stairwell to the attic. When we got to the top of the staircase, Harrison put his ear to the door for several seconds. He looked at us and we both nodded. He pressed his headset and whispered, "On three. One…"

I took a deep breath and slowly blew it out. My mind, my heart, and every square inch of my body were in tune with one another and so ready for this I was tingling all over. I felt adrenaline course through me, and my excitement grew exponentially as Harrison counted down.

"Two…"

I gripped my weapon and tensed my legs, preparing to launch.

"Three!"

Harrison burst through the door, the other agent and me so close behind we could have been his T-shirt. At the same time, the skylight shattered, spraying glass all over, and the FBI agents dropped in on the other side of the room.

"FBI!" one of the agents yelled. "Drop your weapons!"

I knew they wouldn't surrender, and I was right. The men in the middle of the room were already in a heated exchange and scrambled for cover, throwing over tables and diving behind cement columns. A second later, the gunfire started. I dived behind a piece of printing equipment and took a shot over the edge of it, taking out one of Ahmad's men. I scanned the room, desperately trying to find Ahmad, but between all the movement and the haze from gunfire I couldn't locate him.

I heard Ahmad's men shouting and saw two of them attempt to rush the FBI agents in the back of the room. The FBI agents cut them down before they closed half the distance. I saw movement across from me and realized one of our targets was positioning himself underneath a piece of equipment. I dropped to the floor and placed one round in the center of his head.

I saw movement at the back corner of the room and realized a man was climbing up a ladder to a roof access point.

Ahmad!

I ran to where Harrison was hunkered down and pointed to Ahmad as he slipped through the roof access. Harrison nodded and covered me as I ran for the ladder. As soon as I made it to the other side of the room, I tossed my smoke grenade a couple feet in front of me and the thick cloud started to form. I headed up the ladder, Harrison close behind. At the access point, I pushed up the hatch and waited for gunfire. When none was forthcoming, I climbed through the hatch and onto the roof, crouching down as I got my bearings. Harrison popped up a couple seconds later and we scanned the roof for movement.

Finally, I spotted him, slipping over the side of the back of the building. I ran for the corner, hoping I could close the distance before he got away. From the roof, I'd have a clear shot of him in the alley.

My nightmare would be over. My life would be mine again.

I hurried to the edge and peered over but he was nowhere in sight. Damn! I scanned the alley, looking for any sign of movement, then Harrison pointed to the Dumpster we'd hidden behind before. A tiny sliver of shadow at the edge of the Dumpster shifted in the moonlight.

Behind the Dumpster was a wire fence, closing the alley off from an open space between two buildings on the next street. We'd see Ahmad if he went over the fence, but if he had a way to cut the wire and go through it, all bets were off. I didn't even care about the risks. I swung my legs over the side of the building and scurried down the ladder, then dashed for the Dumpster. I could hear Harrison close behind.

I flattened myself against the Dumpster and listened for any sign of movement, but the only sound I heard was the creak of a wooden sign moving in the breeze. I looked at Harrison and held up a finger. He nodded and I began the count. I was just about to lift my third finger when I heard something behind us.

"Drop those weapons," a woman said. "Make a sudden move and I'll cut you in half."

Chapter Twenty

I knew that voice.

Gracie Sampson!

Slowly, Harrison and I turned around, our weapons and hands in the air. The assault rifle Gracie held was no laughing matter. One burst of fire and she could easily make good on her threat.

"You Feds," she said with a smile. "You think you're all so smart, but you had Deputy LeBlanc focused on the wrong Sampson. Brody couldn't run arms. He's too inept. Too nice, especially if he's drunk. Just ask that bitch Celia Arceneaux. Brody would never have slept with her if she hadn't gotten him drunk, and he's never taken a drink since. I made sure of that." She laughed. "The irony is, everyone thinks I'm the nice one."

I felt the blood drain out of my body. I'd encountered a target before who managed a complete split of personalities as Gracie could. The CIA shrink had deemed him a sociopath. No way was she letting us out of the alley alive, and we were too far from the back of the Dumpster to make a run for it. We wouldn't be able to even turn before she blew us away.

"You don't want to do this," Harrison said. "It will only make it worse on you."

"I don't see how," Gracie said. "No one suspects me except my fool of a husband, and he doesn't know anything. Not really. Besides, I'm done with working. Cleaning house is my final performance and you two are part of the dirty stuff that needs to go. Then I'm off for an extradition-free country where I'll spend the rest of my life sitting on a beach and having attractive men serve me drinks."

A burst of automatic gunfire set off in the publishing building again and she smiled. "Sounds like you guys are doing all my work for me. My cousin was useful for his connections, but he's not a good judge of character. He was too cocky...made too many mistakes—the counterfeit money being the biggest. He should never have used those bills until we got the original artist to finish them. Max was never good enough to pull off a job like that."

Original artist? If Max wasn't the artist, then who was?

"Enough small talk," Gracie said. "I've got business to attend to." She trained the rifle on me and smiled. "Bye now."

When the shot fired, I felt all the blood rush from my head. My knees buckled and I fell back against the Dumpster and slowly slid down.

"Fortune!" Harrison shook my shoulders. "Are you hit?"

I bolted out of my stupor and grabbed my stomach, looking for the blood that should be pouring out. But there wasn't even a hole in my T-shirt. I jumped up and looked down at Gracie, who was splayed faceup on the ground, a single bullet hole in the middle of her forehead.

Harrison pointed to the top of the building where two people stood, one holding a rifle, and started to lift his gun when I grabbed his arm.

"They're with me," I said and gave Ida Belle and Gertie a thumbs-up.

Harrison narrowed his eyes at them then shook his head. "The old ladies? Are you kidding me?"

"I told you they weren't your average senior citizens."

He glanced back at Gracie. "Yeah, but that shot from that distance…" The admiration in his voice was evident.

"Ahmad!" I bolted around the Dumpster and slid to a stop in front of the fence. I pushed the cut wire to the side and cursed. "He's gone."

Harrison put his hand on my shoulder. "There will be another opportunity. We're closing in more on him every day."

I struggled to control my frustration. He'd been right there, practically in my sights.

"Gracie!" A man's voice yelled behind us and we ran from behind the Dumpster to see Brody drop to his knees next to his wife's body. "Why wasn't a normal life good enough?" he wailed. "Why?"

I heard footsteps behind us and turned around to see Carter approaching. He flashed his badge at me and Harrison, took one look at Gracie and Brody, and sighed. Then he looked over at us, his eyes locking on mine, and I knew that despite the clothes and ski mask, he knew exactly who I was.

Sirens began to sound in the distance and Harrison turned to me. "Get out of here. I'll handle the wrap-up."

"Are you sure?" I asked.

"You were never here. That was what Morrow and I agreed on." And then it hit me—Harrison was lying. He was never supposed to involve me in the takedown at all. He'd gone directly against Morrow's wishes. Why he'd picked now to defy an order when he never had before was a question that would have to wait for another day.

I handed him my rifle, gave Carter a nod, and dashed for the building, motioning to Ida Belle and Gertie as I went. Ida Belle tossed the rifle over the side of the building and I caught it and put it on the ground for Harrison. I had no idea where she'd gotten it, but I knew she hadn't sneaked it in the coffin. Harrison would have to explain the shot that killed Gracie. Better to have a weapon to back that explanation up with.

I ran down the alley and pulled off the mask before I stepped out onto the sidewalk, then I slowed to a jog until I got closer to the safe house. When I got to the block the safe house was on, I stepped back in a doorway and waited. A couple minutes later, Ida Belle and Gertie came hurrying up the sidewalk.

"Nice shot," I said as I stepped out of the doorway.

I gave Ida Belle a high five before we threw our arms around each other in a group hug. When we finally broke apart, I looked at Ida Belle and grinned.

"If you could have seen the look on Harrison's face when he realized who you were," I said. "It was priceless."

"I still can't believe it," Gertie said. "Gracie Sampson?"

"I know," Ida Belle said. "I feel bad that we thought it was Brody."

"He knew something," I said. "He must have followed her to New Orleans not realizing Carter was following him."

"And Carter didn't realize Brody was following Gracie," Gertie said. "What a big convoluted mess."

"Hey!" I stared at them for a moment, the thought just hitting me. "How did you two get out? And how did you know where to find me?"

They looked at each other.

"We might as well tell her," Ida Belle said. "She's going to see it anyway."

"Oh no," I said. "What did you do?"

"Right after you left, I handcuffed Agent Three to the radiator," Gertie said. "He was still sleeping, so he didn't notice."

"Where did you get handcuffs?"

Ida Belle rolled her eyes. "You have to ask?"

I thought about Gertie's two-hundred-pound purse and grinned. "Never mind."

"I watched out the window to see what kind of car you got in," Ida Belle said. "When Agent Two came back inside from escorting you, Gertie spilled a soda on him, and we locked him in the bathroom when he went inside to clean up."

"Then Ida Belle stole his rifle and we hauled booty after you," Gertie said.

"We made it to the corner in time to see the car you left in turn the corner two blocks over so we ran this direction," Ida Belle said. "We had just slipped into the parking lot across the street from the publishing company when a sedan with four Middle Eastern men drove by real slow-like."

Gertie nodded. "We waited until the car turned the corner, then looked around in time to see them pulling into the alley. We figured they must be going into a building on that street, so we climbed up onto the rooftop of the building next door to get a good vantage point in case you all ran into the street."

"We didn't see the agents on the adjoining roof until they jumped through the skylight," Ida Belle said.

Gertie looked excited. "Boy, that was something!"

"Anyway," Ida Belle said, "we never thought about the fray moving onto the roof."

"Lord help!" Gertie said. "When the gunfire started, I thought I'd have a heart attack right there. It sounded like World War III and then that hatch popped open and that man came out...we dropped like pennies off the side of the Empire State Building. I don't think I've been that skinny in thirty years. I seriously blended into that rooftop."

"Then we saw you and your partner come out of the hatch," Ida Belle said.

"How did you know it was me?"

"Please. We've been watching your moves for weeks now," Gertie said. "We'd recognize you no matter what you had over your face. We're specialists that way."

Ida Belle shook her head. "We saw your tennis shoes. Anyway, we waited a bit to see if anyone else was coming out of the hatch before moving over to the edge to see what was happening."

"By that time," Gertie said, "Gracie had shown up and blown our minds all over again. And you know the rest."

I looked at Ida Belle. "You saved my life. You know what that means?"

"It means you owe me," Ida Belle said. "But I'm not ready to collect just yet."

"Did you get Ahmad?" Gertie asked.

"No," I said. "He was the man who got away in the alley."

They both frowned. "That's what we figured," Ida Belle said. "So what do we do now?"

"We go back to the safe house," I said, "let those FBI agents loose, and wait to hear from Harrison."

"Do we have to go back and let them loose?" Gertie said. "They were pretty mad when we left."

"What about our stuff?" I asked. "All our identification is back there."

They looked at each other and grinned. "We might have left it all in a closet at the bottom of the staircase when we left," Gertie said.

"And we might have rented a car right before that," Ida Belle said. "It might be that Honda parked at the corner."

I looked across the street and saw the rental car emblem on the white Accord parked in front of the safe house.

I smiled. "What the hell? It's not like we can be in more trouble."

Chapter Twenty-One

It was close to 3:00 a.m. when I heard a knock at my front door. We were all sitting in the kitchen, recounting every detail of the night all over again.

"Gig's up," I said and left the kitchen.

I knew it was Carter before I answered the door. Harrison would never risk exposing me, and the FBI agents didn't know who we were, much less where to find us. He stood there for a moment, just staring at me, then slowly shook his head.

"I have whiskey," I said.

"I bet you don't have enough," he said.

"Try me."

I headed back to the kitchen and put another glass on the table. Gertie poured it full of whiskey and Carter sat down and took a long drink. He looked at the three of us, his expression a mixture of admiration, frustration, and slight disbelief.

"If anyone had told me the truth about the three of you a week ago," he finally said, "I wouldn't have believed them." He pointed his finger at Ida Belle. "That shot you made…in the dark, from that distance, and with no scope. That wasn't luck. I know you, and you would never have risked missing and hitting Fortune."

Ida Belle shrugged. "It's just a thing I can do."

Carter nodded. "If that's how you want to leave it, that's okay, but I've done some things myself, so I know the truth."

"What happened after we left?" I asked.

"Your partner, Harrison, gave me a cover story. It was simple enough. I was working with the FBI looking for the Sinful connection, Brody was one of the FBI's suspects, and I followed him to New Orleans. Beyond that, I don't know and didn't see anything until he started crying over his dead wife."

I blew out a breath of relief. That left Carter out of things altogether, which meant any connection to us was weakened as well. "Good. I was hoping you'd be left out of the worst of it."

"Harrison's a sharp guy," Carter said somewhat grudgingly. "Makes decisions quickly, and leave no room for questions."

"He's really built too," Gertie said. "I wish we could have seen his face. I bet he's hot."

Ida Belle kicked her under the table.

"What about the rest of the men?" I asked.

"Harrison said to tell you that none of Ahmad's men made it, so there's no chance your cover is blown since Ahmad never saw you either." Carter frowned. "I'm sorry he got away. I know you were counting on this…"

"We'll get another chance," I said, forcing my voice to sound steady. But the reality was, I was still upset over the lost opportunity and anxious about when the next one might present itself.

"Randal and one of his men were taken alive," Carter said. "Randal was shot but it's a flesh wound."

"And the FBI agents?" I asked.

"One casualty," Carter said quietly.

"That sucks." I hated it when the good guys went down.

"I'll say a prayer for his family," Gertie said.

"Of course," Ida Belle said. She looked over at Gertie, then back at Carter. "What about the agents at the safe house?"

Carter stared at her for a couple seconds, then I saw his

lower lip tremble. Finally, he couldn't stand it any longer and broke into a smile. "I have never seen anyone so pissed in my entire lifetime. When they didn't respond to Harrison's call, we went over to check, afraid something had happened to you. I should have known better."

"I agree," Gertie said. "Maybe from now on, you'll stop underestimating us."

"That's not a good thing," Ida Belle said. "Carter underestimating us is the only reason we've gotten away with most of the things we've done."

Gertie's face fell. "Oh yeah."

Carter shook his head. "Anyway, we uncuffed the one agent and let the other one out of the bathroom. Thanks for leaving the key hanging right there on the wall."

"That door's an original piece," Ida Belle said. "We didn't want you to have to kick it down."

"They both yelled at Harrison for a while, wanting you two brought up on charges, and claiming the bureau would sue for wasting their time, and a whole bunch of other nonsense."

"Sore losers," Gertie said.

"Harrison apologized for the inconvenience and said the CIA would be happy to reimburse the department for any expenses they felt were due. Then he claimed you three were being placed in the federal witness protection program and they wouldn't be troubled by you in the future. They had barely gotten out the door before Harrison sat down on the couch and started laughing."

"And what about you?" Ida Belle asked.

Carter smiled. "Oh, I didn't wait for them to leave. I was too happy to see someone else on the receiving end of your terror besides me."

Ida Belle blew out a breath. "I still can't believe Gracie was the counterfeiting contact."

"Me either," Gertie said. "And there's something I don't understand. Fortune said Gracie said she was cleaning house, but why would she kill Max before he fixed the flaws on the money?"

"Gracie didn't kill Max," Carter said.

"What?" Ida Belle said. "But we thought…"

Carter nodded. "And that's exactly what I would have thought except that after Fortune told me about your suspicions, I checked Brody's alibi for that night. He and Gracie were two hundred miles away at her sister's house for a wedding. It was an all-night party. There's no way she could have gotten back to Sinful, murdered Max, then back to her sister's house without someone missing her."

"Then who?" Gertie asked. "One of Randal's men?"

I looked down at a pile of coins on my kitchen table and like magic, it all fell into place. The coins, the original artist comment Gracie had made, Max's oddly timed return to Sinful.

"I don't think so," I said. "I have an idea…it's going to sound strange at first but hear me out."

And then I told them my theory.

It wasn't even dawn the next morning when Harrison called. Ida Belle and Gertie were still asleep, and since Ally was still at Emmaline's, I took the call in bed.

"Are you just getting away?" I asked.

"Yeah," Harrison said, and I could hear the exhaustion in his voice. I knew that exhaustion well. So many hours without sleep piled on top of a huge adrenaline rush. Then when all that adrenaline left your body, you were ready to collapse.

"Why don't you head to a hotel and get some sleep. Carter

told me everything he knew. You can fill me in on the rest later."

"There's not much more to cover," he said. "The FBI offered Randal a deal if he testified against Jamison. They're pretty sure he's going to take it."

"What happened to Brody Sampson?"

"I actually felt sorry for him. That man was a wreck. Last I saw, he was alternating between telling the FBI everything he knew and crying. Apparently, Gracie and Randal had been tight since they were kids, but given Randal's line of work, they'd kept it on the down-low as adults."

"Did he say how she got involved with Max?"

"He said she gave Max the money to leave Sinful and hooked him up with Randal for work. That doesn't make sense to me, but maybe you get it."

"I do." Gracie was Max's financial ticket out of Sinful. Her way of getting back at Celia for sleeping with Brody.

"Anyway, Max did odd jobs for Randal until Gracie came up with the idea for him to make the coin dies. Brody found a bag of coins. He had some uncle who was a collector and knew they weren't real. He confronted Gracie and she admitted involvement, but said she'd quit. Until he saw Max in Sinful, he thought she had."

"That much might have been true, until her cousin was in the market for a counterfeit artist."

"And Gracie figured she and Max could move up the food chain," Harrison said. "That would make sense."

"Except Max wasn't quite good enough and had someone else do the work. I wonder if Gracie knew who the original artist was."

"I don't suppose we'll ever know, but if I was Max, I damned sure wouldn't have told her. If she had someone better, she wouldn't need him."

"Yeah, she was scary," I said. "If you would have met her before the alley, you would have been really dumbfounded. I was."

"Speaking of dumbfounded, I guess Carter told you about the agents at the safe house?"

"Oh yeah. We had a good laugh over it. I hear you did too."

He chuckled. "I owe you an apology, Redding. I know you told me that the things you got into with them weren't your fault, but I couldn't believe there were people out there more hardheaded than you and who would take even bigger risks. I was wrong."

"God broke the mold when he made Ida Belle and Gertie."

"Nah, he just modified it and we got you. I feel sorry for Carter. He's a cool dude. He doesn't deserve being saddled with the three of you."

I felt my stomach clench. "About that...what's my situation now?"

"I was waiting to call you until I could talk things over with Morrow."

I sucked in a breath. "And?"

"Given that he lost men here and the FBI is looking hard at Jamison and anyone he did business with, neither one of us figures Ahmad is going to maintain a presence. In fact, we both think you're safer there now than you were before."

The breath I'd been holding came out with a whoosh.

"I didn't tell Morrow everything," Harrison said. "I left out the stuff about you and Carter...the personal stuff. If you want to stay, Morrow is happy to leave you there, but if you want to go, I'll figure out something."

Relief, excitement, and also fear coursed through me. I hadn't expected to have a choice, and now, I wasn't certain what to say. I knew it would be easier on Carter if I left. Out of sight, out of mind probably made the whole broken heart thing go faster, and my heart wasn't doing all that well either.

But…

And it was the but that stopped me from packing my bags.

Maybe two butts.

"If it's all the same," I said, "I think I'll stay put."

Chapter Twenty-Two

After a morning celebration because I was staying, Gertie and Ida Belle had gone home, exhausted but happy. Ally was back in residence with me, sworn to silence and tickled that everything had turned out all right. Except for Emmaline, who'd been told the same story Ally heard, no one else in Sinful was the wiser for our latest escapade. We'd explained our sudden return from our Florida vacation as a screwup at the hotel where we had reservations and claimed we'd reschedule for later on.

Ally had gone to meet her contractor, and I had just settled down in my hammock with a beer and a book when Carter walked into my backyard. I sat up on the edge of the strings, watching him as he walked. I hadn't seen or heard from him since the night before and wondered if he'd taken action on what I'd thrown out at him.

His expression was resigned and sad and I instantly knew that my theory had been correct. He pulled a lawn chair over and sat down facing me.

"You don't have to say it," I said. "I can see it in your face."

He sighed. "Belinda confessed before I even started questioning her. Everything you guessed was the truth. When Max couldn't get the design for the money right, he tracked down Landon in the group home in New Orleans. He'd been terrorizing Landon for almost a year before the poor boy finally broke down and told Belinda what was happening."

"Did she know it was Max?" I asked.

"Not until Landon had that little fit in the General Store. She got suspicious and asked Landon if Max was the man he was afraid of. She'd been trying to get it out of him, but every time she asked, he cried and refused to speak for days at a time."

"Jesus. Poor Landon. Poor Belinda. She dedicated her life to protecting her son and then a scumbag like Max takes advantage of him."

"Yeah. She was angry and sad about the whole thing. I don't think I've ever seen someone that broken—a civilian, anyway."

"How did it come together?"

"A shutter came loose and she went out to secure it. She saw Max go down the street toward Celia's house."

I frowned. "I wonder what he was doing there?"

"I guess we'll never know. Anyway, Belinda said she knew Celia was at the church, so she got her shotgun and followed him."

"Where was Landon?"

"At the kitchen table watching movies on his iPad. He never knew she was gone. She followed Max into Celia's house and confronted him in the kitchen. He tried to deny it at first, but finally admitted it was the truth and that he wasn't leaving Sinful without getting what he came for."

I shook my head. "So an angry mama bear was holding a shotgun on him and Max thought that was the way to handle it? What a moron."

"She said she thought he was holding a pistol. She thought he lifted it and that's why she fired."

"Do you believe her?"

"I don't know. Maybe. At this point, she'd say anything."

"Of course. She's worried about what will happen to

Landon if she's convicted. Did you talk to the DA?"

"Yeah. He has a brother with autism and was particularly disturbed with the callousness Max displayed. Charges won't be filed against Belinda as long as she testifies about the counterfeiting. And since she's the only person capable of getting the story out of Landon, they need her with him to build their case against Jamison's organization."

"What will happen in the meantime?"

"They will be put in protective custody until the trial. I think that's what relieved Belinda the most. She and Landon would be easy targets for a man with Jamison's connections."

I nodded. "I'm glad they'll be safe."

"Me too. You know, I'm still amazed how you put it all together. There was so little to go on."

"I'm not sure how I did either. It was a few small things and a general feeling that something was off, you know? I just couldn't figure out why, but then it all clicked. Landon's reaction to Max at the General Store and refusal to draw anymore, Landon's insistence on the sidewalk that day that he didn't like the fake coin, Max's return to Sinful, and the group home that was supposed to have closed down was still up and running. It doesn't seem like a lot, but somehow it made sense."

Carter nodded. "I think instinct is the most overlooked asset of good investigative work. If we paid more attention to those feelings, things wouldn't be as hard to figure out."

I had a feeling that his comment referred to far more than my uncovering of Belinda as Max's killer. I was certain Carter had felt something was off with me, probably from the moment he first met me. And now he was kicking himself for letting his attraction to me override what his gut was telling him. It was a hard pill for anyone to swallow, but especially hard for someone whose job description included reading people.

"Probably so," I said. "But if we didn't get sidetracked by other things, then we would be robots, right?"

"I suppose that's true enough." He stared at the ground for several seconds, then finally looked back up at me. "Have you talked to Harrison yet about your situation?"

I nodded. "He called this morning after he'd had a chance to go over everything with Director Morrow."

"And?"

"And they both feel I'm safer now than before. That given the FBI investigation into Jamison and the loss of his men on-site, Ahmad would be foolish to maintain a presence here. Ahmad doesn't do foolish."

"So you're staying?"

"They told me it was my choice, and I chose to stay."

Carter frowned and nodded. I'm not sure what reaction I'd hoped to get from him, but I couldn't help feeling hurt at his lack of interest.

"Harrison told me how you blew your cover," he said quietly. "Why Ahmad put the price on you."

I felt a blush run up my face. "I shouldn't have done it. All those years of work and I not only blew our setup but got myself put on the top of a hit list. It was stupid."

"It was human."

I sniffed. "Maybe."

"He also told me that you're generally thought of as one of the best agents the CIA has ever had."

"Ha." I looked down at the ground. "No, that honor goes to my father."

"Who Harrison said was a fine agent and also a Grade A asshole."

I felt a lump form in my throat and I looked back up at Carter. "Why are you telling me this?"

"Because I think you're really hard on yourself. Don't get me wrong, in your job you have to be. Perfection is the goal, and the closer you come to it, the better your chance of making it to the next mission. But you can push yourself so hard that you forget who you are or why you're doing the job to begin with."

"I have always known why I do the job."

"To prove to your father that you are good enough?"

I frowned. This was something I'd been doing a lot of thinking about in the past couple days, and the takedown in New Orleans had clarified a couple of things that I wasn't certain about.

"That's definitely where it started," I said.

"And now?"

"Now I do it because I love it. I'm not made for a regular life. Maybe it's because of my father. Maybe it's because I've been doing it for so long. But none of that matters now. The bottom line is that's who I am. I need the work, the thrill, the excitement, the challenge."

Carter nodded, and I could see the disappointment in his expression.

"I understand," he said. "But it's not something I want in my life. I came back here for a simple life…"

"And all I offer is complication."

"I'm sorry, Fortune, but whatever we had can't continue. The two of us want completely different things. When I left Iraq there were things I never wanted to be part of again. Your job…" He sighed. "I can't sit home wondering if you're all right when you're gone. That's not the way I want to live."

I felt the tears well up in my eyes. I understood exactly what he was saying, and I didn't blame him one bit. But it didn't hurt any less.

He rose from the chair, leaned over, and kissed me on the

cheek.

"Good-bye," he said.

I felt the tears run down my cheeks as he walked away.

Maybe I'd made the wrong decision. Maybe I should have left Sinful and started over somewhere without the baggage. Without the heartache.

I wiped the tears with the back of my hand. Carter was only one part of my life in Sinful. All the others were worth staying for. I just had to keep reminding myself of that.

My cell phone buzzed and I looked down at the display and smiled.

Crisis at the café. Celia's struck again.

What's next for Fortune Redding? Find out in FORTUNE HUNTER, coming 2016.

About the Author

Jana DeLeon grew up among the bayous and gators of southwest Louisiana. She's never stumbled across a mystery like one of her heroines but is still hopeful. She lives in Dallas, Texas with a menagerie of animals and not a single ghost.

Visit Jana at:

Website: http://janadeleon.com
Facebook:
http://www.facebook.com/JanaDeLeonAuthor/
Twitter: @JanaDeLeon

For new release notification, to participate in a monthly $100 egift card drawing, and more, sign up for Jana's newsletter.

Printed in the USA
CPSIA information can be obtained
at www.ICGtesting.com
LVHW021557221223
767236LV00003B/127